PROVIDENCE

GIRLS

ISBN: 978-1-7331699-3-6

Book cover art by M.E. Morgan

morlevart.com

Interior design by rafael nicolás

beacons.ai/nicosraf

First edition 2023

Content Warnings

- Past sexual abuse between a father and daughter
- Past rape
- Past traumatic pregnancy
- Body horror
- Emetophobia
- Body dysmorphia
- Ableism toward people with albinism
- Mentions of suicide ideation

1. VIN, 1948

Dear Azzie,

The night I escaped my hometown, all those years ago in late 1932, my heart crawled into my convulsing throat. It was November 1st, after Papa and the townsfolk planned the All Hallows' Eve sacrifice: me.

There must be no point in speaking to someone who's been gone for fifteen years. I doubt if I put my letters in a bottle that you'd find them. Still, I've been told that reflecting on the past can clarify the future.

Here is how I fell in love with you and almost died. Not in that order.

Though, I suppose, the Lavinia I was perished. *I* sacrificed her and what she loved, a quiet life with her two odd sons.

I'm not sure how I survived the journey from Dunwich to East Providence. Don't remember every individual day.

By leaving, I betrayed the promise of my flesh, that invisible, cosmic birthmark that says: You were born to be sacrificed, like a goat. Hung upside down and gutted. Put on the pyre to crumble to ash. Eaten by worms.

I ran off through meadows of honeysuckle and wild strawberries. Whip-poor-wills promised to follow me and, as a hummingbird drinks nectar, suck out my soul. As if that was a worthwhile bounty.

To my shock at the start of my escape, the little birds' devil-lullaby faded. Faded. And as I write this, I can't help but laugh myself to tears again. My ribs hurt, nicked and worn down after thirty-six years.

All my life, I was told I'd hear their warbles until my last breath.

If I tried to flee, I'd end up like the golden-haired lady in the Tennyson poem: dead. But I could never die beautiful enough for an oil painting. My sadness, even today, has never been the stuff of those books you showed me. Ophelia with a golden halo and a crown of rue.

I refused to give the whip-poor-wills my soul. Enough of that. My heels slapped the dirt floor, and I fled into the unknown. Twenty-six hours away, or so the books say, was nothing an automobile couldn't easily cross, but for a girl in a town of three-hundred, where only three families owned autos, it was as if I crossed an ocean.

For days, many deliriously sleepless, I jaggedly went southwest of my childhood hills and mired through briars and frosty wetlands until, no surprise, I ended up in more wilderness. My cuts bled and stung.

I languished there. Fed on what berries and roots I knew were safe from Papa's botany books, the ones I wasn't supposed to read because they weren't written for a woman's mind.

I endured the sun, how it mercilessly peeled and blistered my skin; I was careful to hide in the shade, and I relished the overcast and rainy days. For the first week, I slathered myself with a greasy mint uncture I made for my condition.

One night, when I curled in the leaves and slept among fleas and aphids, I looked up at the stars and begged my "husband" for guidance. I couldn't understand him if I tried.

Sometimes, I found a mossy place to sit. Perched myself against a birch tree, so nothing could sneak up on my back.

As the bark scraped up my spine through the rags of my ruined dress, I breathed a sigh of relief.

Cold seeped into me. A bulbous wound throbbed on my foot. Leaked pus and blood on a rash of red and orange leaves. And I laughed because I was dying and ready for it. It didn't hurt.

Hell, after what happened to me, what Papa did to me, nothing hurt as bad.

I rested against the tree and promised myself death, since that was how I knew how to be gentle to myself. All I had to ward off the night was a mouse-eaten shawl that reeked of mildew and rain. I was soaked to the bone, except for my chapped lips.

I leaned my head against the bark and let my eyes flutter closed. The last thing I saw was the single amber sputter of a firefly.

Once, I was a girl, Azzie. Even in my mid-thirties, that was what I was. Old Mad Wizard Whateley's girl. I accepted it.

Otherwise, they called me an idiot hick, plain white trash only worth pitying or disposing of. Hateful words. As they would say, the simple hillbilly. The twisted albino, that hateful, defining word, like all my family before me.

I gladly took the first label: girl. Innocent, crystallized in the fuzz and smoke of stories by our meager hearth. Mama's white hair, the same color as Papa's and mine. Even as old as seven, she let me drink from her by the fire. My chubby hand grasped the coarse linen of her apron.

Mama kept me close, so close, not letting her humanity run dry in me. I didn't understand until I gave birth myself. If she weaned me before one of the villagers split the crown of her head with an ax, I might've lost her. I had the memory of her milk, mingled with woodsmoke, when I needed to sleep.

I lost her, and I lost Wilbur, my smallest son, when he warned me of my fate.

My teeth tilled dry skin off my lips. "Sorry, m'sorry." Mucus poured from my nose. I needled my forefinger against the inside of my elbow, where there was already a set of thin, pink oval scars.

If only I could sleep, but when I opened my eyes, two black, shiny globes sized me up.

My fuzzy vision became sharper, as it often does when fear pumps my blood faster.

A bear cub regarded me with curiosity, though my sluggish brain imagined myself as an inviting honeycomb. I snorted, and it looked like the mass of fur and muscle bristled, offended.

Were bears scavengers? Yes.

And was this one eager to start early on carrion? Maybe.

Or had I died and this was a psychopomp, like the whip-poor-wills, ready to take me to the Plateau of Leng with its satyr-men and pomegranates or the ethereal onyx spires of Kadath, which glittered above a white wasteland? He was my Hades ready to kiss the spring from my mouth before he let the Styx snatch me away.

No, by then, my spring was long gone.

If only, I thought in the months ahead, but now I am glad I didn't die that night; before I met East Providence and before I met you. God.

I knew I hadn't died, that if I died, Papa might not miss me. He wouldn't, but Wilbur would. Sweet Wilbur, who waltzed with me in the rain, as spring slicked the dogwoods and made them drop their snow of delicate petals. Before he came along, I tasted thunderstorms alone.

The cub came to sniff me, its nose damp. I froze, unsure if this was a dying vision or the land of the dead.

How could I ever be frightened by something my biggest son could easily swallow whole?

For what felt like minutes, it overwhelmed me with the damp scent of its fur, twinkling with dew and rain.

And then, it left me, rustling to my right. The bushes yawned open, and then it was as if the cub never existed, except for the prints it left in the mud.

Gone, but its presence stayed. I wasn't safe there, and worse, I was awake. So, legs like planks, I slogged off to another copse of the woods, where I shriveled against an alder, too exhausted to shake or weep. My left shoulder, where the fabric tore, prickled furiously from brushing against poison ivy.

I plucked some wineberries and ate them, sucked their red off my fingers. They were delicious. They were strange to this place, like me, strange and bloody. The trees looked at me differently.

Thing is, berries weren't enough. Living off stale, half-molded bread and cold lentil soup, I figured the berries might've been more nutritious than wheat loaves with white slime on the ends, but they didn't fill me up. I was hollowed out, low and scar-streaked breasts dry after my twin sons were born.

Funny that I survived so long in the mud and earth. I huddled under shade. Left only to forage or drink water from streams, which I slept near because the rush calmed me. Roamed past trees of blue moss; purple, glittering mushrooms dappling the fallen, white trees; and stars, neverending stars.

By my bare feet, two cats ran in circles, never catching each other. My husband, whose face I couldn't picture, hugged me, and I buried my face against the supernovas on his collarbone. He, great and unknowable, would make me worth something again. Easy lies.

Peace until, naturally, my body rioted. If I could be born again, I wanted to be something small like a sparrow or a mouse. Something that could live off so little and die easily. In the wild, mice live for a year. Sadly, they dream.

Eventually, one morning, the world went outside-inwards. I knew I was weak, but I didn't know I was dangerously weak until my brain flickered. Too late. Blue and brown shadows goldened. Greens blackened. And I collapsed.

I'm unsure if I should continue because this sounds awful dramatic. Not the words of the girl who lived in the shed on Hound's End Street, a dirt road in a solar system of milkweed and honeysuckle. Learning poetry and eloquence has been a long battle, but a worthwhile one.

Eloquence. Oh, fuck it all, you know I'm only stalling before I open the nightstand beside where you used to sleep, before I cut the twine and tear open the parchment to read what you wrote to me all those years ago.

Don't read my letters, you told me, don't read them until you've lived.

Am I ready? My heart has always been ready to be full of you. I've worked to revisit the past, so I might bury it.

2. AZZIE, 1933

VIN:

Here it stands, my account of the beginning of this condition, a horrid blessing.

How strange it is to write with you lying beside me as my nurse.

I hate that word. You'll never believe it, but as a girl, I never let Father take me to a physician. How dare anyone say I needed fixing in any way.

Times have changed.

Indeed, I want to catalog my condition. For whatever reason. Perhaps if I'm ever discovered, a hungry scientist can pluck me apart and read these entries I've typed on the top-of-the-line Model 3 Olympia, imported from Berlin. I don't see the point, since there's no cure. Maybe this is for myself, but I've never cared to be self-indulgent. Overly, that is.

Who knows? A long-lost paternal relative may come by, and this will be all that's left of me. Me, the last of the Waite bloodline, and my mother's kin? That's another discussion. I am less ashamed of her and her line.

Not much physically has changed. Tired, sweating, hot flashes. Only every few days. When you tried to serve me bluefish or rice or johnnycake, I thought I might vomit, but I did eat some anyway. I can walk around fine most days. At night and the late morning, my back aches.

Vin, if anything happens to me, I'm leaving this cottage to you, so you can give any stray relative this account as a memento, a warning. Ah, I haven't even put a date. I was never good at diaries or letters or whatever this must be.

If I'm too tired, if I remember, I might need to ask you to type one for me, though I hate to ask you to do anything. Your company and friendship have been enough.

And I'm unsure if I have the courage to show you these papers yet. If I asked, you wouldn't read them, but I can't shake my worries of judgment. Of unsettling you as you're adjusting to this new life. Nevertheless, hunching over a typewriter with this new, unidentified back pain is labor.

I can't start from the beginning because it's awful, and I've told everyone I don't remember those hazy twelve years, since I was thirteen. A lie, always has been. I felt everything, but it's too painful. Even now, a chill skitters down my back, like waking up to a hundred spiders creeping on my skin, this cursed skin I'm never allowed to know as mine.

No need for melodrama. Maybe that's the fever.

Anyway, if I don't start now, I never will, since the later stages of my condition will make my fingers clumsy.

What strikes me now is when I met you, last year in 1932. I never allowed myself to be introspective before that. Sentimentality? That was to be shunned, always. No one could be let in. I silenced those specters that exist only as echoes to assuage loneliness.

I could never go home. Mother? No, not even if she's still in that attic with the veil over her squamous head. No way in a thousand soggy hells would I ever let her know what happened to me. When violence happens to us, and we tell others, don't we commit violence to everyone who wants to keep the peace, to keep those sweet images of those who turned out to be monsters?

And Father? He was the first I silenced.

So, when I learned of this property my family neglected, since it was nowhere near as vast as Father's estate, nor did it have any of his scholarly or esoteric texts, I was relieved to have a home outside of Massachusetts, though it's not as distant as I would've liked.

Nevertheless, in an economy such as this, I am surely fortunate to have a home that belongs to me. Not quite a seaside cottage, but in East Providence, it's a sea-adjacent one.

One main floor and an attic, with a stone chimney and wooden exterior, framed with a green roof, a small porch in the front and a larger one in the back. I had the lead pipes replaced with iron, and all was well.

Quiet, and when the quiet grew toxic, I purchased a radio to half-listen to dramas through interludes of static.

With everyone thinking I'm dead, all loose ends are dealt with, and I can be free.

Vin, why is it so much easier to write this as if it's meant for you? Here I am, saying more than we did that first day you arrived.

You must think I don't trust you. To be perfectly honest, I'm not sure if I did trust you when you first came here on that pleasant autumn morning. When a cat sees a shadow, after the torpor of its long, selfish solitude, it startles.

So, when you came into my life, an unknown factor, it wasn't personal to you when I flinched and skulked away. It felt like it, and I hope things will be better. I'll be better.

When you first came here, came here, as if I didn't enlist the help of the Nicks brothers a two miles away to carry you in and set you on the spare bed, so you wouldn't freeze to death. When you came, the air promised rain, and the yellows of the leaves were browning.

There I was at the kitchen sink, washing a plate, that one with the blue flower buds around the rim. Outside the window, the bath towels on the clothesline fluttered in the wind like ghost hair, and the hammock swayed beneath a curtain of swallow-wort and bittersweet nightshade.

I set the plate down and looked at the newspaper on the counter. More post-examinations about the election between Roosevelt and Hoover; Roosevelt won.

I didn't need to be outside to know that the day was perfect, reminiscent of my pre-adolescent days when I'd sneak cigars from Father's study desk, the drawer right under the taxidermied squid, and go to the docks. Lazily watched the gulls circle above. Listened to longshoremen banter. An old, rain-stained sign announced proudly in a curling script, *The Harbour*.

At home, the tastes of salt and tobacco intoxicated me. Plastered to the plank by my left boot was a newspaper ad for a Paulina Fredrick talkie, you know, the one where she's Joan Crawford's mother, and an age-reducing soap.

If I looked out far enough into the sea, Devil's Reef poked out. As alive as the water was, it was hard to believe whispers that my home was a dying town, barely even a village, since the water was everything.

Shocking to think I stood there without the wind smacking me into the water, with what a pale wisp of a girl I was, this acrylic smear in the ocean's green reflection. A hellion who set my own diet, I subsisted off toffee bars and coffee ice cream; I was stubborn and argumentative, and Father would chastise my unladylike mannerisms.

"Quit stomping around, Asenath," Father always snapped at me, lowering his bifocals to glare. He smelled like cigars and old paper and something sour.

In the uppermost estate window, with its yellowed curtains, Mother, even under her thick silk veil, stippled with turquoises, must've seen me leave, might've seen the cigar I slipped under my gray coat, but said nothing when I'd go to the attic to visit her. She was the one person I'd tell things to.

And now, you.

You came in late November. The days darkened early. None of that slow easing from rose-pink evenings to twilight.

With the breezy day only a little overcast, I decided to stroll through the woods and listen to birdsong. You're better with birds. And cats. And everything. Back at the hamlet I called home and outsiders called cursed, when I clattered my feet on the cobblestones and ran past rows of gabled roofs, there weren't any strays. Animals have never liked me, and in my childhood town, only gulls whorled over the houses, picked scraps in the streets, or screamed.

I found you in the clearing, collapsed facedown on the forest floor with your white hair dulled from rain and mud.

And I jumped, heart in my throat. Stood too long in surprise.

I knelt by your side and turned you over. It wasn't easy; you were so frail, but I've never been strong.

I was afraid to hurt you.

Even now, I cannot believe you're almost forty. Because when I saw you, I thought you were a girl younger than me. The world made you so small. And god, you looked like you'd been sucked into the undertow and thrashed about. Spat back out.

Leaning forward, I set my head against your chest, felt the pulse in your neck with my fingers. You were breathing, slow, deep.

I feared leaving you alone. What if you were a vision, and the Nicks brothers thought I was mad? What if you died while I was gone? After some deliberation, with the bones in my wrists and ankles popping, I went for help, but not before I draped my coat over you.

After I ushered the brothers to where you were, thankfully, you were still there. Not a mad dream. They brought you to the spare bed at the cottage, a twin layered in dust.

If I knew I'd find you half-dead, dear, I would've cleaned it. The leaves and dirt smeared on that bed like menses. Or bridal blood. We agreed to burn your old dress and shawl, once you could bear to look at them.

I despised doctors, yes, I'm sure you've recognized that by now. But I let one of the brothers phone Dr. Phillips, so he might save you from death. I crossed my arms and waited.

When the doctor came with his thick-lensed glasses and wisp of a black mustache, he observed you, lifting your wrist to feel your pulse and inspecting the angry pink burns on your nose, cheeks, and forehead.

"Has she woken up?" Phillips asked me.

"As you might see, she's asleep." Having company irked me.

"I mean between finding her and my arrival."

"No."

"And you simply found her in the woods?" he asked.

"Yes, facedown."

"She's an albino," he said, in what felt like a non-sequitur.

"Yes, obviously." For one of my heritage, the dark-haired, dark-eyed witch-seed from a sleepy hamlet, you'd think I'd learn not to be so dry. Men could get ideas.

He prickled at that.

I was meant to go, oh, you're right! Or oh! What's that? Vin, you know me, so sensitive and timid. I'd never intentionally wound a man's ego. A pure accident. Naturally, he was the maven, and I was the unlearned girl of twenty-seven years.

Going to the curtain by your bed, he drew it closed. "She'll be sensitive to sunlight, and it's likely she cannot see well. Or perhaps hear well. Regardless, the best thing for her now is bed rest."

"Bed rest?" I asked. There, see, I gave him a chance to expound his knowledge and expand my meager mind.

He regarded me blandly through his dark eyelashes. "Yes, a long period of staying in bed. A month, perhaps more."

I looked over you, your burns. "And once she improves, what then?" Having only known you like this, silent and hurt, I didn't know what to expect if you woke up, and the unexpected was dangerous. Unacceptable. Didn't matter if there were good unknowns.

Grief. Disaster. Love. All the same. Those unknowns might unearth truths I worked to repress. I deserve not to languish in the past.

His thick brows knitted together. "What do you mean?"

"She must have a home. Somewhere. I hope I'm not expected to keep a vagrant." I'm ashamed of what I said, the judgment. Not even half a year ago. For almost half my life, as a child, I lived with good fortune and little discipline.

Why, this present morning, you fell asleep beside me by accident, and you'll apologize, I know, and I never wanted to care for you at all. I'd constructed my own lonely garden and routine.

Eat breakfast at 6:00.

Leave home at 6:30.

Start work at 7:00.

Go home at 2:00. Arrive at 2:30 or 3:00, depending on traffic.

Fill the space between 3:00 and 6:00 by fiddling with the radio, reading, or fidgeting with the typewriter. Gardening. Attempting a poem or two. Then, sigh. Smoke a cigar. Resign myself in defeat and abjection.

Eat dinner at 6:00. Opium, maybe.

Bathe.

Lie down in bed at 8:00. Opium, definitely. Pray to fall asleep by midnight.

Any disruption irked me: my nerves disrupting my sleep; the pangs of hunger if I forget to bring an apple to City Hall as I sort files.

I ate at the right times or not at all; all baths were in the evening, so they wouldn't detract from any other activities. Staying in the tub too long wasn't healthy for my wandering mind.

Phillips said to me as I grew somber, "We must first let her recover before we send her back to her family, her husband, or children. If she goes back at all." He gave a shrug. He was only here to ensure you weren't dead. Women disappeared sometimes, and their fathers and husbands were never questioned because what they did with their women was their business. "And it might be good for you to have company." The last word came off a tad bitter.

I suppressed a scoff.

"Then, I'll see that she's cared for," I said, gripping the bedroom doorknob hard, the threshold where I was the sentinel. You might think it's humorous. Even in my weary reluctance, I stood there to ensure you were okay, that the doctor did nothing untoward. As a nail, I saw hammers everywhere. "What do I do about the sunburns on her face?" Will aloe work?

"Ensure that she remains indoors and put lotion on it, particularly with aloe." He stepped close to me, and I kept my back to the door.

"Careful," I told him, and he coolly maintained distance, albeit without so much as blinking. He didn't know how perilous he made this feel, pinning me down with his stare.

With a curled hand up, like a good inquisitive doctor, Phillips asked me, "Miss Waite, how are the tinctures working for you?" No matter what I think of physicians, of him, I need the laudanum.

"Good. I've slept well." I never liked the way he looked at me and wanted him to leave. I always felt he was ready to have me sent to a hospital ward for nerve exhaustion or hysteria. The sour recluse, the spinster.

"I'm glad to hear it. Let me know when you need more from the pharmacy," was his only reply, rubbing the side of his face. He picked up his valise and left before I could go to my reticule and pay him for the inconvenience.

I feared leaving you alone or sleeping because I might wake up to my clothes and pearls stolen or a knife at the pulse in my neck. All that. God. I hope you know I don't see you poorly, quite the contrary. You, gentle Lavinia, right here with some of your hair on my clammy shoulder, where sweat has soaked through the linens we'll wash.

Because I was so used to fear, I was scared of you.

If I could, if it were proper, as I sit here with the typewriter by my side, teetering close to the edge, I'd brush the hair from your eyes. Smooth away the twitches and whimpers.

You don't mind my ugly imperfections. The sweat, the fear of getting close. How I bristle and slink off in silence. My eyes, which men always feel free to comment on. *Beautiful woman, if only those green eyes weren't so overly big and shrewd.* All the more to eat them with, but these too-big eyes never bothered you.

Yet. We'll see.

But. No. After what you went through, I can only ever be a mild horror to you.

My heart did ache at the sight of you, but pity wouldn't increase your survival odds.

That's what I told myself.

I left to get you a glass of water.

3. VIN

IF I OPEN THE NIGHTSTAND DRAWER, I CAN READ EVERYTHING you wrote long ago. You said I could, but it feels invasive. An admission that I miss you. I've moved on and lived, but I see parts of you in the garden of bleeding hearts and orchid primroses.

The lilac quahog pearl by the lamp, the most beautiful thing I own.

Own. As if I can possess even a small piece of the ocean. As if I can fool myself into thinking I have your heart against mine.

Enough. I need to keep my distance. This is what moving on is, isn't it? I cannot languish in the past.

No. How odd. To let it go, I must face it. I must imitate the books I studied with you by the fireplace.

If you were here, we'd give ourselves each other, but for once, I am doing something for myself without searching for reciprocation from anything or anyone. A person, the cosmos. Growing up, all I wanted was for Papa to love me because when he loved me, he left me alone. Leaving didn't occur to me often because I concerned myself with making him happy in the hopes of changing his disposition toward me for good.

Perhaps I'm fooling myself, but I feel less heavy, having written what's already here. The stack grows thicker, shares my soul. To think I'll be rid of the memories is naive.

I want to try.

The first days of November had passed in hunger and fear. When I awoke in the spare cottage bed, mud caking my legs, floating circles of teal and scarlet muddled my vision.

I struggled to adjust to the yellows and browns of the room, cold replaced with warmth. When I waded through miles and miles of the wintry bogs and salt marshes strewn across the border of Massachusetts and Rhode Island, it was all a wash of black. Sun-faded blue. Rheumy gray.

My eyes were often smudgily unfocused, especially around the edges, but my senses grew acute in my desperation.

The sheets around my legs clamped close like a carapace. My bones hurt less.

It took me minutes to realize I was in a bed, but when I realized I didn't recognize the room, relief and panic poured into my stomach, neither and both at once. Relief that, upon looking at the white shade of the lamp and a nature oil painting of a lake, I was not back home.

I hadn't been caught by Papa or any other men in my town.

Thank the gods of beyond.

My hope didn't last. My heart beat like a rabbit's because I'd been captured by a stranger, or strangers. Taken to a place without my knowledge or consent. For all I knew, Papa would walk in wearing his violet robe with ropes in his hands. The shuttered window gave a feeling of smallness and imprisonment.

Dry mucus crusted my nostrils, but I smelled the hearth woodsmoke in the other room. And in the corner of the bedroom was what looked like a witch's broom, and yes, I recognized the three-foot cinnamon sticks, wrapped in twine. To rid ourselves of the damp odor, Papa and I would make these. It was set by closet doors built into the wall, panels of wood embraced by the wallpaper.

Otherwise, the room was barren. I was alone.

Until the stranger—that's you—came in and stood by the door. A charcoal sketch, your brows dark and prominent, arched in observation. My heart leapt to the roof of my mouth.

You regarded me warily, like I was a thief who sneaked out of gaol and plopped messily into your life. Like I always set my back against bark in the wilderness, you kept your back to the door.

You weren't the one whisked off to a strange place, but I fully believed you feared me, maybe hated me.

It was then I figured out that we were similar somehow. Maybe it was providence. With the callous way the universe worked, which I learned firsthand with my spine digging into the splinters of a mildewed table, I didn't believe in soulmates. It was never fated that we be hurt like we were or for us to believe those pains defined us right down to our marrow.

We are not stains our fathers smeared against a paper they crumpled into the dustbin. Just as you have a mother, so do I, and whatever it is inside us that is like a soul is connected to neither of our parents.

One might think our souls are lonely, but that's like saying a bat is lonely when its squeak lets it see a cicada through space and time. We may never see each other again, but I know we're kindred spirits. We were.

Azzie, you were tall, though not as tall as me, I realized later. Whereas I was messy, my hair crinkled and tangled and oily, you were composed. A dark straight line, a slash of graphite against the yellow wallpaper. The part of Papa's drawing compass that jams into the wood and stays there. Stable.

Funny then, that you were the one to leave for good, like the pencil that bends farther away while the center holds.

Did I trust you? No, but then again, I'd lived in a crumbling, mice-infested cabin with Papa. How could this stranger be worse? You were a stone between my past and the future.

"I suppose it'd be stupid to ask how you're feeling." Yes, that was you, even at your most distant: self-effacing and wry. You held a glass of water, and my dry throat throbbed in need.

I gawked, lips stinging, only to realize I must've looked stupid. Even burned, tired, muddy, and half-dead, I worried about what Papa would say if he saw me. I forced myself to sit straight up and keep my mouth closed.

You took a step forward to set down the glass of water you made me. And I tensed.

Perceptive, you caught it immediately and stopped. Guilt flooded me. All you wanted was to give me water, but I was afraid.

A gulf brimmed between us, and I couldn't see if it was darkness or light, whether there were fish or stars.

"May I wash myself?" I asked you. "D'you, do you have somewhere where I can clean myself?"

"A washroom?" you asked.

"Well," I replied, unable to help myself, "I certainly wouldn't want to bathe here in this room."

Your jaw worked. "Yes, the door is out here past the kitchen. And if you come out now, I can..." You trailed off, but you looked as if you wanted to say something else. Offer to help me up, perhaps.

Strangely, as tired as I was, I had an acute burst of energy. When our eyes met, you gave me a nod and left. I heard a clink from the other room, the glass on a wood surface. Odd that you took the water with you, but not so much, knowing you now after all this time; you were so flustered that you bustled away without thinking.

I waited and listened. The need to relieve myself throbbed below my stomach, so I fumbled out of the bed, my feet twisted in the sheets I'd sullied with mud and sweat.

As fast as I tried to be, the world crawled.

Pausing at the door, I shut my eyes. If I could face Papa for nearly forty years, I could face you, a stranger.

No, I was the stranger.

I could do it.

So, I crossed the threshold.

Outside the bedroom was a small kitchen with one wooden slash of counters and a white icebox for perishables. To my right, a living room with a burning hearth. My eyes ached when I saw the fire, and I flinched away. Lone atop the mantel was a burnished antique clock. Your grandmother's on her father's side, you told me once without elaboration.

The walls were also yellow with white and red roses vertically peppering the expanse. Behind the plush green recliner and leather sofa, opposite of the fireplace, were rows of oak bookshelves, completely stocked. And beyond all that stood two doors perpendicular to each other, both shut. The front door and your bedroom.

Between the kitchen and the living room, set against the wall, were narrow stairs that I learned later led to the cobwebbed attic with family mementos, grainy photographs of an aunt and her gap-toothed son, who were long-dead, so you ignored them.

The dead were best forgotten; I discovered that was how you felt. You longed to forget while I've been cursed with remembering.

I never asked if you knew them well, if they were also victims of your father or your cursed town. I meant to, but time went by too fast.

As I oriented myself and went to the brown door that led to the washroom, I left a messy trail of dirt and leaves everywhere on the wood floor. I was reminded of the streaks of afterbirth I left after I gave birth to my twins.

And when you, sitting by the hearth, saw it, you looked so very tired. The side of your mouth twitched. Your shoulders lowered, and you ran a hand through your hair.

Instead of feeling sorry for you, I resented you for seeing me struggle and standing at a distance. I was the one who ran almost nonstop through water and woods. And because I'd only known my own pain, which was shameful and ignored, I could only see the world through that.

As I took you in, ready to shout or simper, that was when I noticed something.

I saw the first glimpse of one of your pale, horizontal neck scars; with how your bangs hung down and how swiftly you fussed with your collar, I only noticed two of them on the left side of your neck.

I said nothing. After all, I had silver stretch marks on my breasts, stomach, and thighs, and I'd hate for them to be pointed out.

And no one's scars are nobody's business, I decided.

Though we'd already met, I also noticed how you were dressed for the first time. White, buttoned shirt and black slacks. Suspenders. Men's clothes. I'd never seen a woman wear pants in Dunwich.

Too different, we were too different, as wrong as that impression was. Different and the same. Me, with my crinkled white hair and pale, dreamy purple-pink eyes, and you with your sleek black hair and dark, ponderous green eyes, shining like agates.

Anger lost, what I did do was shrink and say in a tiny voice, "M'sorry."

Simper it was.

You blinked for the first time. How funny it seems to think of the first time you blinked at me. Then again, there came a time when your eyes swelled so much that you could no longer close your eyes.

"Why are you sorry?" you asked, standing cautiously. If only you knew how impossible that question was with the mounds of regret settled on me. Sisyphus had his boulder to push, and I had the mountain.

Really looking at you without all the shadows, I noticed for the first time how much smaller you were in height and how big your eyes were. I don't mean like in what few ads I'd seen of movie dames, ingénues. They looked big for their sockets. Instead of making you look young, they made you look on guard. Alert. While my eyes saw too little, yours saw too much.

Nevertheless, your eyes were the most beautiful ones I'd ever seen, and that hasn't changed.

"You don't need to apologize to me," you said roughly, but your tone only provoked more guilt. Already, I messed up. Failed. Didn't belong again.

My shoulders tensed, and I resolved to pronounce my words better, even if it meant speaking with a staccato. "I'm sorry. I didn't mean to make a mess." I learned long ago that the best way to keep others from staying angry was to whimper and withdraw into myself.

To try and convince you that I was genuine, I stepped forward, and your shoulders squared, prickled.

"Don't." You opened and closed your mouth, struggling to form the next words. You rubbed the front of your throat, as if in discomfort, and then your hands dropped to your elbows.

My bottom lip trembled, and then so did my hands.

Sorry, sorry, sorry.

I now know that for you, you received apologies like a body would accept unknown substances. It rejects them because they're unfamiliar.

"Don't apologize. There's some aloe and mint lotion on the counter," you said, "for your..." You circled your palm in front of your face. My skin stung so badly that I thought I'd molt.

Before I went into the washroom, I took the glass that you placed on the table and, tongue swollen and like sandpaper, gulped down all the water. It had a residual metallic taste, but the coolness refreshed me. When I set it back down, I was a little dizzy. Afraid of being clumsy and stupid in front of a stranger, especially this curious one, I scurried to the washroom, which was small but bigger than the one at home.

Rather than wood, it had tiles, and the tub was porcelain instead of a vast copper basin for bathing, cleaning dishes, and washing my hands. No, there were bathroom and kitchen sinks for that, on their own stands. The light had already been turned on. The faint scent of lemon chemicals permeated the air.

Bigger. That was a constant theme of the cottage, and the emptiness yawned around me. After I peeled off my clothes, I turned on the water and quivered in wait, too conscious of only a door between us. When I looked down and saw my pale toes against the speckled foam-green tiles, I grew dizzy.

Green. vibrant. All my dresses and shawls were white or the off-white of mildewed curtains; dyed garments were a luxury. I treasured what color I did have in my life, a quilt Mama made for me when I was in her belly, a rough patchwork of rose pink and foam green.

Back home, gone.

Lost.

Admittedly, after spending weeks soaked in rain or water from bogs and salt marshes, I was reluctant to stew in a tepid bath. The need to get rid of the crawling in my scalp and on my arms was stronger than that feeling. Steam rose from the rising water, but it didn't register with me what it meant as I shut off the faucet.

When I warily stepped into the tub, afraid I'd fumble with how weak I was, I shook and gasped. The water in Papa's one-story farmhouse could never be this hot.

My head bobbed, my crown sliding against the porcelain. And while it ached at first, that steaming water did the trick, was what I needed for my sore body.

I wondered if comfort like this was what babies felt in the womb. If I could, I'd fold in half and let myself be submerged in the water. That and the birdsong of tiny sparrows and kingbirds lulled me to sleep. Different birds, gentler songs. That didn't cajole me, beg me to die, so they may feed.

And like coming into life, I jolted when a knock on the closed washroom door harshly jarred me awake.

"Hello, are you all right in there?" you asked, tapping on the door, voice muffled by the boundary between us.

I took a few seconds to orient myself, my chin submerged in the water. "Y-yes." As I sat up, the water sloshed violently, some of it colliding on the tiles below.

The water, almost black from the grime I shed, had cooled. My nipples were painfully stiff. Goosebumps prickled my arms, legs, and breasts. On my breasts were deep, pink half-moons scars darker than the skin they circled. I feared anyone seeing them.

"Wait," I called.

With the taut silence that followed, I would've thought that you left if I didn't see your shadow under the door. "Yes?"

I croaked, "How long have I been in here?"

"An hour," you replied.

"Oh."

A dull thud behind the door. I imagine you, coiled into yourself, going to nervously rap your knuckles against the door and realizing your mistake. "I've set a gown you can wear out here on the display table."

"Okay. T-th..." Before I could get my thanks out, your shadow left the crack under the door, leaving me to shudder in the dirty water.

Dozing in the tub, I felt like I'd gotten away with something, stolen away a moment for myself like I'd sneak cookies out of the oven, only to be caught and reprimanded by Papa, who often told me I was bloated and grotesquely fat, as I struggled to ever be girlish again.

By then, hell, I was closer to forty than twenty. I was too old to pretend to be a girl. And too undreamily sad.

For most of the day, you left me alone.

4. Azzie

It was two days after you came into my life that the skin around my neck "scars" started to peel.

If I didn't fear it'd be hurtful humor, I would've joked that contact with another human, you, gave me an allergic reaction.

Even when we were strangers under the same roof, I couldn't imagine how I'd feel once I went to work and left you alone by yourself. And, Vin, I didn't realize how slowly the wonder you saw in everything seeped into my own view. The way your eyes widened when you saw my auto or my small garden.

For so long, even as autumn raged one last gasp, everything was a swamp of brown and gray. I lived in a forever winter. If you asked me what color the City Hall sign was, I couldn't say, despite passing it five days a week. I might've said white. Was the bubbler in the grass before the steps or to the right of the entrance? Or the left? I couldn't remember.

The past didn't darken my world; no, I, and only I, grayed it out because it was easier. If I acknowledged the vibrant colors, the scarlet tomatoes on the market stands and the mustard-yellow sundresses dancing in mild summer afternoons, I might've mourned what I couldn't have. It was stupid.

I have a new life now.

So, I let it all go. The ocean, when you first glanced upon it, to me was nothing more than a muted blue. Dead indigo. But only when your eyes widened and your arms flew open did I see the shuddering cerulean.

That particular evening, we both saw more than we bargained for.

I hate myself for how aloof I've been toward you. I don't even know if it's proper to ask forgiveness for a sin I'm afraid to acknowledge. If I admit I'm cold and unable to be loved, will you see the truth and leave me? Maybe that'd be best for both of us.

If I were to ever go out into the world again, I wonder how the colors would further change to me, if they'd be even keener. If I'd work to love the world more, appreciate my co-workers' timid smiles and small talk, trace my fingers along the feathered petals of the daisies that peek out of the sidewalk cracks.

Despite trying to be stoic and rational, I think these things about flowers and colors, but I can't voice them outside of writing. Lyrics in the head, no poetry outside of it. For so long, I told myself the verses I adored weren't meant for the world. They were meant to stay inside pages, like secrets.

And then, there are simple, silly things. The first time you drank one of my coffee cabinets, and you had a little milkshake mustache from it.

Why, why can I never fully show myself to you? You've brought color into my life, and this is how I repay you.

Finger cramps. Fever's bad today. Jaw, back hurt. Neck's on fire.

Will try to say more tomorrow.

5. VIN

I was surprised when I huddled into the spare bedroom and saw that, in the time I'd napped in the tub, you had stripped the bed and put new, striped sheets on, and a pomegranate-red afghan was folded at the end. Blissfully sleepy and unable to think much, I slipped in. And that bed was too comfortable and warm for its own good.

I burrowed into the covers, tugging the afghan over me.

Nothing disturbed me, and though a dampness lingered in the cottage, and water stains darkened the ceiling, it was nice to not have rivulets of rain water trickling down the wallpaper when a light drizzle came and lulled me to sleep. My wet hair was soft on my cheek.

A whirring yanked me out of sleep, but by the time I could keep my eyes open, it faded. And then my eyes closed again, and I dozed a little longer.

Later in the evening, I poked my head out of the bedroom like a baby crab surveying the darkness outside of its developing shell. You were at the dinner table, which shone in the candlelight. The scent from the candle was spiced and pungent. You sipped on a glass of water.

"Thirsty?" you asked.

"What do you have? Water?" I asked, and I hated the burning in my cheeks and neck.

"Yes," you replied with a touch of wryness, "but I also have something else."

Tentatively, I sat across from you, elbow on the table. I ensured my eyes stayed on the wood, on my stubby fingers, nails bitten to the quick.

Unlike the sharp and jagged lines of my old furniture, and unlike the dramatic angles of the rest of the cottage, the surface had a rounded, smooth edge. Like the chairs, cushioned with feathers, it cost money.

You rose and offered me a frothy brown drink already on the table, which was heavy on the syrup and served in a vodka glass.

You sat back down and continued to sip your water as you picked up a book with its cover peeled behind it like a twisted arm. I couldn't catch what the material was, though the lines on the pages were short. Verses.

Part of me said accepting food and drink from a stranger was dangerous. Most of the people in my life needed something from me. Needed to take something. I expected that you were the same. And if I couldn't give anything, I'd be thrown out.

After giving birth, though, my idea of peril was different. I'd been sitting on the ground as a bear sniffed my cheek and didn't feel the same anxieties I did in motherhood.

Whether I'd die in childbirth, which was seen as an inevitability.

Whether I could even properly care for a child when all I knew was being afraid.

I sucked on the green straw with vigor. Usually, I was more careful of how I ate and drank around others.

The taste surprised me, and I paused. With the color, I might've guessed the milkshake was chocolate, but it wasn't. I loved the taste, the sweetly bitter taste of coffee and vanilla on my tongue.

"What's in this?" I asked you. "What's it called?"

You kept tracing your forefinger along your nails, which were meticulously cut and smoothed. "A coffee cabinet. Milk, ice cream, coffee syrup. It's like coffee milk with vanilla ice cream."

Coffee milk, like putting milk in coffee? I'd never heard it said that way because, frankly, I had no idea what you were talking about. I didn't travel far, but once one goes from an isolated, poor town to a coastal city, things are different. Back home, my diet largely subsisted on farm animals, squash, rye, pumpkins, and beans. And in bad years, stale or moldering bread.

Unlike East Providence, my town didn't have much in the way of seafood, or international dishes. And yet you would introduce me to the world of fish and your favorite: lobster.

"Do you have more?" I asked you, lightly raising the empty glass.

"Hm. Yes." I caught your steady eyes under those dark eyelashes, the lids heavy. "I forgot to ask. How much syrup do you like?"

"I..." I thought about it. "I'm not sure."

You went to the counter to the blender, a contraption which I'd never seen before. And when you plugged it in and dumped your concoction inside, you turned on the blender.

When I heard its hellish racket, I froze, jaw locking. I'd grown used to alertness at new sights and sounds, right from when I heard my babies' yowls.

You released the button, and the noise stopped, the building froth lying still. "Should I stop?"

Already, my mind had gotten used to the sound; it was familiar, even if I didn't like how unapologetically metallic the blender's screams were. "No, go ahead."

You waited a few seconds, but I didn't change my mind.

Once you finished mixing the coffee cabinet, you set it on the table, careful to keep your distance.

"This is delicious. Thank you." If I forgot to thank someone or apologize, Papa would threaten to cuff my ear.

You nodded. "Don't drink too much or it'll affect your bathroom habits." You stared below my nose, something like amusement glittering in your eyes.

"Experience?" I rubbed my hand above my mouth, wiping away the foam.

"I've cut down." One of the first non-answer answers that revealed more than you thought. Digestion troubles, coffee-induced jitters, insomnia. You carefully controlled what you ate and drank, grew used to eating and drinking in tiny, moderated amounts.

"Are you going to have one?" I asked.

"No. Not this late." You idly rapped your knuckles on the table and, looking down at your hand, stopped, stretching open your fingers.

I started, "I, I've been meaning to ask...how did I end up here?" I doubted you could carry me a long distance. Then, at least.

"I found you and had the men who live nearby carry you inside," you answered crisply. "Interesting question, though. I was going to ask you the same thing."

A lump formed in my throat. "Thanks for saving me."

You swallowed thickly, cupping both sides of your water glass. "You don't have to thank me."

"I already did."

It amazed me how composed we were in that time, how we'd trained ourselves to suppress and hold everything in. I realized there was a reason babies scream when they're born.

With your long fingers, you gestured to your nose in a loose circular motion. "Is there anything more that can be done about your skin?"

My nose itched, but I didn't dare touch it. Best to let the flesh peel. "I'm 'fraid that's genetic."

Your hand eased on the table. Everything beyond your wrist was covered, but I couldn't help but admire how nicely shaped your fingers and knuckles were, how delicate. Mamie Bishop, my only friend at home, had well-contoured hands, too, as callused as they were. What was it with me and other women's hands?

"I mean the sunburns," you replied. "Something quicker than the mint. I'm afraid I don't have anything but generic lotion."

"That could work." At home, I used mint, aloe, and primrose oil. "Do you grow any primrose flowers?"

"In the winter, and they flower in spring. I should go to the store and retrieve something. Just looking at the blisters makes me wince." Your expression was impassive. How hard it was to believe then that you were anything but impenetrable.

Never had I let the threat of the sun stop me. Sitting alone in the dark all day like a vampire in my mossy castle wasn't the most uplifting exercise. The rush of the wind in grass, the rain tracing veins down my back, the heady scents of pollen and dogwoods, the sweet honeysuckles and the sinfully red residue of seeds when the wild strawberries gave me their tart blood, I needed them all.

Where are we? I wanted to ask you. The shuttered windows maddened me, even if they protected me from sunlight. As I looked at them, I admired the art on the walls, oil paintings of lighthouses, foaming waves, and sea storms. I wondered if you had anything I could draw with.

I asked, "What's your name?"

You blinked. So caught up in what should be done, what was necessary, that you forgot to introduce yourself.

"Does it matter?" Not confrontational, but curt.

"I, y'know, it's an awful lot to take in. Wakin' up in a place y'don't know. Not that I'm ungrateful." I swallowed, embarrassed at the slurry of words that spilled out of my mouth. My knobby hands were shaking.

"I understand." Then, I doubted you did, but turns out I was wrong. "Have you ever read the Bible?"

I shook my head. "No."

"Neither have I. At length, anyhow. My father kept a copy I would sometimes skim through." You set the side of your head against a fist. Deliberating.

To give your name was to give up another piece of yourself to someone else.

I chewed on my already ruined lip. "You don't need to tell me if you don't want to."

Your eyes widened a fraction, but you averted them. Reluctance. I gave you an out, a choice. Then, I didn't realize how precious that was.

"My name is Asenath," you said, and it was as if, instead of the floodgates opening, they cracked a sliver. Your voice dipped and rose with the syllables, as if you were getting used to your name again.

Asenath. A proper name, it felt like, ancient and respectful. Lady Asenath of the cottage in the woods, the dark-eyed dame of East Providence. An arch figure in black lace inside a yellowed gothic novella. Heroine, or villainess.

"I'm Lavinia." It sounded strange rolling off my own tongue. Back home, most people called me Vinny or Lavinny. When they didn't call me the albino slut or the inbred freak.

Ugly, no-chinned Lavinny Whateley and that goatish brat o' hers.

A light of recognition flickered in your eyes. "Ah, like the woman in the Shakespeare tragedy."

My heart dropped. I'd hoped you wouldn't know that one. "'Fraid so." Papa thought I was too dense to pore over the mildewed plays and understand them deeply.

Your lips thinned. "I'm afraid I should be the one to apologize, then, for our unfortunate names."

I scratched the side of my scalp. "How is 'Asenath' unfortunate?"

"It means 'peril' and 'misfortune'. Also, 'belongs to her father'." Your lips curled in distaste. According to Papa, I thought, all daughters belong to their fathers. Despite all he'd done with those ink-stained fingers and rose-lilac eyes, my eyes, I thought of him often, not always unkindly. After all, he raised me, and so often, I compelled myself to make peace to the point that it felt ingrained in me to trust him.

You continued, "'Lavinia' is a pretty name, no matter what happened in literature."

"Thanks. S'pose I don't like bein' named after a lady who was silenced."

"Not entirely. She found a way to speak and get revenge on the men who wronged her. It wasn't conventional, but she used what she had." You looked down at your glass of water, knuckles whitening. "If you want food, there's some in the icebox. I could make a plate, but we must take care to clean them. We have mice."

You clasped one hand over a fist and squeezed.

Like me, you also struggled to understand your position in conversations or your body's place in the moment. As if we had a puzzle spread before us, but long ago, we weren't even allowed to be pieces.

Then again, my body always had someone else's hand trying to fit it where they said it belonged. Papa's. The gods. But I at least had Wilbur for regular conversation or Mamie Bishop, a distant friend.

Your limbs were stiff and as angled as the walls around her. When our eyes met, I detected a twitch, a suppressed smile stamped out; I'd no idea what I had done.

Turns out, I'd given myself a nice coffee cabinet mustache. To my surprise, you stood up in one fluid motion and went to the front door, almost going out of it.

"Wait," I called.

You stopped and looked at me. "Yes?"

"It's getting dark. Do you—do you keep everything off at night?"

You gave me a curt shake of your head. "No. I cannot stand complete darkness."

"Oh." I was relieved, and as I sat there, you left. I didn't hear the auto start.

Momentarily alone, I went to the washroom. When I saw that mustache in the brass-lined mirror, I wet my hands and scrubbed my face so hard it ached; the peeling skin, flaking off on the porcelain, burned. My elbow knocked into a glass bottle I hadn't noticed on the counter, and I saw the label. *Aloe: for skin reparation and anti-aging.*

Afraid to use what wasn't mine without permission, I righted the bottle and left it alone, even as my skin hurt. I went out into the empty house, and how void it was took hold of me. Like at Papa's farmhouse, my lack of control grew consummate as the shadows lengthened.

Since it was evening, and the canopies of trees let wide shadows yawn over the thin, browning grass, capped with the hair of leaves, I wasn't afraid of going outside. Always, there'd be sunlight. Even at night, the moonlight was merely taken from the sun.

Despite myself, my mouth gaped open at the sight of the auto, which was a newer make than anything in my hometown. A 1930's wine-crimson Plymouth with a long snout; to me, all vehicles looked vaguely insectoid, like the Mi-gos I read about in some of Papa's books. Before, I didn't care for autos. The smoke they expelled smelled rotten and metallic, and their growls and purrs were awful loud, like industrial lions. They made me jump. I couldn't imagine living in a big city, fearing these giant metal beetles that could easily crush me underfoot.

Your vehicle, though, your second feet, your escape, was beautiful, like you. Meticulously cared for, like you. No rust or busted lights, and I imagined once it came to life, no toxic black smoke poured from its gullet. My hand hovered over one of the silvery headlights, and I imagined them being turned on and being as prismatic as oil on water. The reflection of my palm, splintered, moved like mercury. Like the eyes of...

I went cold and snapped out of it, chin jerking up. Hazily, I took in the exterior of the cottage. It had two heads, two points that rose high and almost seemed to be removed and imperious toward the rest of the cottage.

The cottage wasn't decadent, but it was bigger than the home Papa and I shared. This other place, even so close to where I'd once been, similar in weather and temperature—indeed, it took some adjusting to breathe in it. Always, I achingly struggled to find how I existed in the world.

I glanced around the corner, around the auto, and I glimpsed a hammock of white knots tied to a wooden frame, which swayed with a light gust, and the clotheslines, where pins kept the sheets I'd marred. My cheeks once again went hot.

When I looked back toward the dirt path, the thriving garden, I saw you, a small black curve on the dusk- and lantern-lit earth. Walking closer for a better view, I recognized mint, garlic, lavender, lemon balm. A sea of yellow and green, dashed in sun-pink, and then a spatter of scarlet: wild strawberries, where you knelt. Gentle but efficient, you added mulch to the garden from a cloth sack. I inhaled the earthy scent, augmented by something sweet.

That was, until you paused, as if the wind gave you a hint of me. Your head darted up, right where I was. With how unmoving you were, you could've been the oil painting where I slept, that deceptively frozen and innocent sea. You didn't so much as blink, wary. You reminded me of a startled rabbit, except for the striking green of those large eyes.

Caught, I shuffled my feet in the dirt and approached you, though I kept a few feet between us.

"Do you need something?" you asked, expression schooled, but I saw the skin pinch around your eyes.

"Can I help?" Even though I'd never gardened, I'd read so many books on it, and my fingers twitched. You looked as if you wanted to cross your arms, but with the salmon-pink gloves caked in dirt, it would've been too messy.

You hesitated. I'd surprised you, and I liked doing that.

"Yes." Your lips thinned, sucked away for a few seconds. "If you want." You were never hateful toward me, but you could be curt. Even if I resented it then, I don't blame you for being guarded anymore. Besides, social cues are hard if you spend most of your time alone.

I knelt across from you and inhaled the scent of the earth, pungent and soft with night petrichor. To me, it was odd someone as prim as you unabashedly knelt in the dirt. At home, it was easy to tell those with money from those who didn't. Clothes that fit, sleeves that weren't scuffed at the wrists and elbows. Hands, whether they were soft or callused. Despite sitting closer than we had all day, you were galaxies away. I suppressed a hum in my throat.

Gesturing to the strawberry plant between us, you said, "They thrive near the coast a little too much. More and more, new strawberries bloom each year. There were many by the sea, at home."

"I love strawberries," I replied.

You kept your attention to the ground. I felt invisible. "They're enjoyable. Mostly, I sell them. I've never been one for overly sweet things. I tend to like a hint of something else, bitter or mild. Like chocolate with toffee." A pang in my gums; I loved toffee, too, but it hurt my teeth. "I thought I wouldn't like this hobby, but it's efficient."

"Do you like cinnamon?" I asked you, thinking of the cinnamon broom in the corner of the spare bedroom, which I hadn't yet thought of as my own.

You rested an arm on your knee. "It's my favorite kind of scent, sharp, overwhelming. Back home on the coast, it masked the smell of fish that was everywhere."

"Yes, I imagine."

"It was so small, too, essentially a village, not like Arkham. Smells carried."

"I've always wondered what Arkham was like."

You rolled your shoulders. "Not a big city by any means, not like Boston northeast of it. With how small my birthplace was, it might as well have been an ocean." Many of Papa's books were copies and forgeries of tomes from Miskatonic University, right on Arkham's river valley. "But anyhow..." You lapsed into silence.

I struggled with the temptation to restart the talk. Before I could think of a topic, something that wasn't an apology, we finished and went back inside, not touching once.

The first night at the cottage passed uneventfully, though when I woke up, pale light streaming through the teeth of the shutters, I realized I'd bitten my lip hard enough to taste blood.

I was comfy in the old-fashioned gown I wore. It was faded and a little big, and I wondered whose it was before.

Later, we sat in silence at the dining table, eating a savory lunch of lemon-peppered salmon and rice; I'd never had salmon before, but you made it perfectly.

I set my fork down, trying to tease a grain of rice off my teeth with my tongue.

"Where are you from?" you asked. At my hesitation, you held up a hand. "You don't need to say."

I shrugged. No point in hiding. Dunwich wasn't much of anything. If I said the name, I doubted you'd recognize it. Most folks who lived there, even me, didn't bother much with calling it by name. Two syllables that melted together. Most outside folks said it wrong anyway. "A small town northeast." Town, we often said, we're going into town. There were only three-hundred people there. I don't think nobody knew much about the place if they didn't live in it.

You straightened in your chair. "In Rhode Island?" While it took some fumbling for me to get to the point, like water circling the drain, you merely stated it. I decided to try brevity.

I forced myself to talk slower, so the pronunciation of the state didn't become mush on my tongue. "Massachusetts."

A light flitted across your eyes, though you controlled your expression. Not even a single tic. "I'm from Massachusetts, too."

The world grew smaller, and I imagined myself as less alone. Not a stranger traversing a plain of my own, light-years away from any other breathing soul, but in a realm of circles I'd never dared step into. Maybe I wasn't a pariah, and maybe I belonged and deserved as much as everyone else.

Those thoughts didn't flourish, but they stuck, seeds shaken from a fox's coat.

"Really?" I couldn't hide the surprise, the hope, in my voice.

"I never knew much about the places outside of my little town on the coast." My home was about an hour from the ocean. A shiver went through me, realizing how close we were before we met. To think it was fate, well, that'd be absurdly romantic for the universe we live in. Not like the gods divined grand love stories with blissful endings.

Wonder in my voice, I leaned forward and asked, "You saw the ocean?" As much as I tried to imagine the glimmering waves of blue, tried to hear the rhythmic thrum of the tides, I couldn't.

"Almost every day," you said.

"I've never seen it." Desire, a craving I couldn't pin down. The ocean was its own beast, like petting the rippling fire-pelt of a tiger.

In my dreams, I'd seen cozy, gabled towns and high black spires and writhing trees speckled with blue fungus. Moon-creatures shaped like toads and the size of hills. Beings with bodies like wires and vertical mouths and eyes a color I couldn't name. The strange? Usual to me, but my own world? The sea? Locked away. A dream. Long ago, I accepted the bizarre and cruel as normal and gave up on the mundane and kind.

You must've seen the misty look in my eyes. "We don't have to travel far to see it here."

"Oh, I know." I ruffled, not needing to be told that. I wanted to know more, but I hated how stupid I must've looked for my age.

The idea of gazing on the vast sea, where the Dead Ones dream in the eldritch poems, intoxicated me. The sky fascinated me most, walking under the umbrella of planets and stars, Venus and Orion. Even wanting a normal life, I wanted to be important. Transcend what I'd known.

I caught you scratching at your neck, flakes of dead skin falling under your fingernails.

"Sometimes my scars itch," you explained.

I cocked my head. "You look like you have gills."

That was when I had my suspicions about your condition based on my readings, but a part of me refused to believe I'd gone from one otherworldly scenario to another. A boring domestic life sounded more divine than divinity, even if being taken into the stars was a stone of a dream settled in my lungs, that promise of purpose.

Not only purpose: belonging. Finally knowing I'm home.

"Do I?" Your eyes dulled, shuttered. Too soon, you were withdrawing from me.

My throat swelled.

You were the only person in the world I had, so I worried that I offended you.

Eyelids fluttering, you sighed. "I know you didn't mean anything by it."

I said, both to you and myself, "Maybe I did." I'm not sure. Even if I didn't know I felt it, I realized I could talk back without worrying about being called an idiot or being slapped.

You straightened your shoulders. "I'll need to go to work tomorrow."

I blurted out, "Do you need me to leave?"

You stared. "Why would you think that?"

Pursing my lips, I said, "'Cause it's your house, and I'll be a stranger alone in it."

My reasons weren't selfless. Not entirely. I was so, so afraid of being by myself in the cottage, and the fact it wasn't mine only salted my fear with guilt. What if Papa and the townsfolk came and dragged me back home? A mildewed cloth in my mouth, ropes scraping my wrists.

Thinking of the shed, that night, I almost locked up.

What if Wilbur changed his mind after he disobeyed Papa? I wouldn't put it past Papa to force him to come fetch me as punishment.

Despite not being altruistic at this moment, I didn't want to take advantage of your generosity.

You said, "I only ask that you leave my room alone. I have my typewriter there at my desk, and I'm afraid if it breaks I cannot afford a new one. You can use the radio." You jerked your head where it sat in the living room, right under the front window.

"Aren't you afraid I'll break that, too?" I asked, petulant.

You didn't blink once, your stare intense. "Here, I'll show you how it works."

The radio was a beautiful piece of work; it still is, though it long went out of use. It was a rectangle composed of walnut with two big, black knobs below what I thought, then, to be a massive compass, a number with a long white needle. On the top left, the numbers went 170, 150, 130, 110. From the middle top to the right, they went 90, 80, 70, 60, 55. On the bottom was, from left to right, 500, 400, 300, and 200. To me, it was a bunch of zeroes.

You showed me how to use it, and I was startled when it crackled to life with Bing Crosby. Then, I tried, fiddling with the knobs.

You gave a little shrug, which I found too endearing for our own good. "I don't use it often, and the dampness here has a way of getting to the electrical things if they go unused too long."

The day passed with no incidents, and I slept. That was when the trouble started.

In my dream, the world was completely dark. I walked and called for Papa and my sons. Unspoken words buzzed in me, angry gossamer wings in the gummy black. I looked down at my stomach, and it was swollen and full.

No wonder, I thought with dream-logic, no wonder I couldn't find my sons. I pushed a tentative finger into my swollen skin, and the cosmos shoved back, my belly taut with bumpy stars.

Light flooded the world. Poured white as milk down my legs.

I awoke, eyelids gritty, in a field of black sunflowers. My arms stretched out, my body spread out on my back. And when I rolled my head to the right, a wide black eye stared lifelessly at me. A pink tongue. A dead cow. I cried out and froze. I needed to move, but my limbs were ice.

I always loved cows and goats, but I especially loved pigs. The sows, in particular, loved any affection they could get. When I rubbed their spotted snouts, they'd snort happily and roll on their sides like dogs, so I could pat their fat, pale stomachs.

But when I peered across the field, all I saw was grisly death. Hooves, feathers, everything. Dismembered. Skin atop mounds of eyes and loose jaws.

I'd landed in the slaughtering grounds where I belonged. While I was pregnant, in the plunder of sadness, I accepted I'd die in childbirth. I should've. Right in the ground, if my death kept me whole enough. Papa already got around to pricing coffins. Cardboard's cheapest, he told me over cold, bitter coffee with a dead fly bobbing in it, belly-up. Ever since the shed, he refused to meet my eyes.

Hopelessness made me docile, pliable to whatever the gods'd do to me. Who'd miss a girl no one wanted around, useless except to bear a god's children?

As I sat there, the air shuddered, and I saw eyes, my eyes, and something I couldn't see ate everything, crushed it all and slurped the jellied guts into oblivion. I tried to scream as shadows fell over me.

I shook, shook, eyes snapping open in bed. Trembled and trembled as mucus poured from my nose. It tasted salty.

Weight blanketed my shoulder. A hand. Your green eyes centered the world above. You were dressed in a simple white shirt, partly unbuttoned, and rumpled black pants.

"You were screaming," you said softly, once I'd stilled.

A hot wetness between my legs. I'd leaked a little in my underwear. Not enough to stain the gown or sheets, but enough to feel ashamed. My cheeks grew hot in humiliation.

Thankfully, you straightened and took a step back. The last thing I needed you to know was that I pissed myself. Since I got pregnant, my continence was manageable, but weaker. Especially when nightmares came.

"Bad dream," I said, breath shuddering and visible. I was still on my back. "That's it, that's all, that's all." You went to the closet and folded a blue blanket over the crook of your arm.

Setting it at the end of the bed, over my feet, you murmured, "I take laudanum to keep from dreaming. Maybe one spoonful will help."

Again, you gave a part of yourself to me without complaint. Did you realize that you offered so much of your life to me? You gave me access to your radio, offered poems and books. Oscar Wilde and Sappho and Tennyson and Baudelaire. No restrictions, no demands.

Maybe like me, it wasn't entirely selfless. Finally, you had company, and it felt good to give. Share. Allow yourself to exist in this space, little by little.

In my panic, I shot up, leaned forward. Gripped your hand. A reflex.

Startled, you jerked it away like I'd scorched you. Another reflex. Hurt tears swelled in my eyes. That chasm ached in me, the hollow in my stomach that Wilbur and his twin once shared. As excruciating as the conception, pregnancy, and birth were, so long as I had at least one son as a friend, it was all worth it. I had my reason to get up every morning.

Your face contorted. "It's not you." An explanation. She stared down at the floor.

A sour taste in my mouth. Sick. Hurrying out of bed, knocking my shoulder into you, I fled into the washroom; fell to my knees; and vomited in the commode. The rustle of fabric. Bare feet padding on the tiles.

Here I was, a white-haired, stupid girl of thirty-six, of piss and bile, of nothing.

You followed me at a distance. "Here, do you need help?" Even without touching, I felt your heat behind me.

I shook my head, hair strewn on porcelain. "I just need to bathe. Be alone."

"All right. I'll bring you a change of clothes." My bleary eyes fell on you.

You left me, and indeed I bathed. And indeed, when I opened the washroom door in only a towel, a nightgown was on the display table. Shame flooded me, leaving the other crumpled, sullied gown on the tiles by the tub. Papa trained me to always pick up clothes.

When I eased back into bed, you reappeared like an apparition. Sauntering to my side, you said, "Tomorrow, we can go see the ocean, if you'd like."

"Won't you be at work?" I asked.

You waved a hand, holding a spoon in that one and a brown laudanum bottle in the other. I wondered dryly if she even set it or the opium down. "I'll be home in the afternoon." That wasn't what I meant.

"Afternoon?" I scratched the inside of my elbow. Not enough to draw blood.

You blinked, and I saw a glimpse of how young you were; despite being the eldest here, I always felt more girlish. "Is there something wrong with the afternoon?"

I touched my arm. "The sun hurts my skin because, y'know."

You raised a hand to your face but didn't touch it. With the spoon, you looked funny. "Does the aloe help any?"

"Yes."

"Maybe I have something. I make things out of the plants outside, and while the primrose isn't ready, I might be able to make something else."

I didn't want you to go through any more trouble. Anyone who cared for me treated it like a burden, an obligation. Except Wilbur. Did I make him feel like he was a burden to me? "I can tolerate that. I, I'd like that. To see the ocean. But can we wait until it's a little darker?"

You blinked. Shutter, unshutter. "Good. Yes. Though, I'd rather we not go when it's too dark. It'll be cold, and I don't like the dark."

"All right." I asked you, "When you're gone, can I read some of your books?"

Your eyes widened a little. "Yes, of course."

Dryly, I asked, "Surprised I can read?" No thanks to Papa; that was all Mama.

When you shook your head, some of your hair fell in your face. I wondered what you'd do if I brushed it back in place, but I didn't dare. "No. I didn't expect that question."

"What did you expect?" Our little cat-dance of asking questions, of being pulled close and then apart. You opened your mouth, and color speckled your cheeks and throat. Granting you mercy, I said, "I'm only joking." Your shoulders softened. I worried my lip. "I know where I came from. What I am. Lavinia is too pretty a name for someone like me." A creature, Papa once called me. "Papa was smart. Our family, it was a good one once, before it became poor white trash."

The shake of your head was almost violent. "You aren't trash."

"What am I?" I asked you, sad.

"I don't know. I don't know you well. But not that." You fidgeted. Self-conscious, and you uncapped the bottle and precisely filled the spoon. You handed the spoon to me, and determined to show you that I could function, I swallowed the bitter laudanum without spilling any.

I didn't want you to leave. As scared as I was of touch, I craved it. The idea of you kissing me and telling me that you'd never leave me, never abandon me, well.

My cheeks and throat were hot. Bad thing about my condition is that I can't hide a blush. Thank goodness darkness exists.

Too bad the lamp was on.

So, there I was. Embarrassed by my vulnerability, there in the gown you lent me. Which I realized exposed the outline of my nipples. I flushed as I handed back the spoon, and I kept my elbows close to my chest.

"I hope it'll help," you said.

"I hope it will, too. Thank you."

You hummed to yourself. "When I was very young, Mother would come down and rub my back. Her hands were very damp, but her being there lulled me to sleep."

You took some time after that to speak. "I'm not sure I'd be good at being anyone's mother. All right, pretend I'm your friend." I wasn't as nervous under your constant gaze. You weren't used to thinking when to blink or when not to stare. Besides, I learned long ago that unnerving others could be a blessing of its own. Because I was a pariah, I could dance in the meadows with only Papa's demands and tasks on my mind. No one else's.

I wasn't sure what to do as you knelt by the bed, so I slid under the covers and, horizontal, turned away from you. When you touched my back through the gown, it was light, but I opened my mouth anyway. Releasing a slow exhale. My chest ached.

Your knuckles glided between my shoulder blades and caressed my spine. That touch sent a chill across my entire body, and my shoulders instinctively clenched. You paused. You rotated your hand, and your fingers brushed against me.

"Do you want me to stop?" you asked in a gentle rasp.

I muttered, "No, please don't."

You continued to rub my back. As you massaged my untensing muscles, my eyelids shuttered. You hummed a whimsical note under your breath, and I imagined the hammock outside swaying with the high and lows of the tune. To the movements of your hand and the cadence of your voice, I started to drift.

A sea shanty, you told me later, a song from home.

6. VIN

WHEN YOU CAME HOME IN YOUR BLACK SKIRT AND WHITE blouse, we ate a small early dinner of fresh, grilled tuna from the fish market and rice and talked little. One hour passed and then a few more until the sky outside darkened. I figured you forgot about our ocean talk and stood to slink back to the bed you'd lent me. Odd how welcoming a bed could be when it wasn't my own, the cold and bloody one I'd had since I left the bassinet.

"Do you still want to go see the ocean?" you asked me as you took my plate to clean. It felt wrong to have someone else do chores. I nodded. "All right. Let me change first. I shouldn't be long." Change. But you were already beautiful.

After you changed out of your work clothes, you were different, dressed in your white shirt and gray suspenders and slacks. Instead of being a bad different, it drew me to you more. Maybe you didn't recognize these unveilings, when a rosebud starts to lets its petals peek out—

Yes, we've reached the stage of roses. This was when I didn't know I was truly lost in you, but the world had that softening, that haziness narrowed by mysterious anticipation.

Truly, when I think of it, you were maybe more like a funereal white lily. Ghostly, somber, and tense, with petals that are thick as parchment and not quite as easily bent. Closer to flesh.

You were also like a lily with their male-female parts, in that you occupied the two spaces effortlessly. Like the color of the sea, of your eyes, you were liminal, human and inhuman. On the precipice of dying, like I once believed all women were: spring and autumn, death and the maiden.

If you noticed me gawking as I stood up at the dining table, you said nothing.

Your hand jerked toward the door in an ushering motion. "It'll be quicker to go by auto."

I swallowed thickly and grinned as I slipped on a faint green coat. "Yeah, I figured." You blinked, hands slipping into your coat pockets, and turned on your heel.

As I followed you outside, I noticed the grass was now brown. White flurries spiraled down as if rotating on invisible spindles. Not enough of a force to show on the ground. Though winter hadn't come, some of the ominous trees were almost nude, leaves abandoned like old selves. Papa once told me trees will prematurely let their leaves yellow and die for self-preservation. Still, most of the trees were a rash of deep crimson, apricot, and gold.

When I slid inside the auto, the leather seat was more comfortable than I expected in something so mechanical.

Once you got inside, after you turned the crank, I ran a finger along the passenger side handle. "I've never been inside of one of these."

"Hm." You nodded once. "What do you think?"

"Smells different than I expected." Not as rusty and metallic. Mostly, I caught the heady musk of leather. Besides the smoke and salt, you also had this deep and heady fragrance I couldn't quite name. You: tobacco and pine and salt.

You asked with a curious arch of your brow, "A good or bad different?"

I stuck my tongue against the side of my cheek in thought. In a little town, all that was different was seen as bad. But that meant I was bad, and so was Wilbur. "M'dunno."

When the auto started to go, rumbling all the while, I almost fell into the floorboard, and you stopped.

"Are you all right?" you asked me, a catch in your voice.

"Yes, yes," I said, straightening myself. Through my hair, you looked like you were suppressing a laugh, and I realized I must look funny. For once, I wasn't embarrassed.

We sat together in a silence easier than it should've been.

My breath frosted the window. Papa didn't like when I breathed on the windows of our tiny house. It sounded absurd when I thought about it, but he criticized my open-mouthed breathing, my trembling hands. Any smiles or laughs when I was in the same quiet room as him were suspicious because he assumed I must be thinking of a joke at his expense. If I thought something bad about him, I stomped it down for fear his magic sensed it.

As fragile as I was with my albinism, or as fragile as Papa said I was, even though I was like him, I could offend him without saying a word. I wondered if you went through something similar with how aloof you could be.

I wiped at the cloud with my sleeve. The window squeaked, and the fog started to fade.

"Don't worry about it," you said lightly.

I set my back against the seat and muttered, "All right. I s'pose I won't."

You treated the auto well, washing it whether the windows or frame needed it or not. I must've looked like a child realizing that breath mist exists in autos, too.

I didn't feel like a child. I felt old, grasping for more memories before I die. Because even if I'd escaped death, that was my fate. We all die, but some are destined to be ritual meat.

That was where my mind was at. And it was okay to me because I had these two contradictory ideas in my head, but they made sense to me in their cohabitation:

–I am worthless. Chine bone to be sacrificed at the altar. Nothing without my purpose. I need it.

–I'm worth something because I'm meant to transcend my fleshy prison. All the roles forced on me—daughter, godswife, mother—have given me a purpose. Which is good because I'm nothing without my purpose. I need it.

This is life. To be on the periphery, a weak flame waiting to be snuffed out and forgotten. But if I'm a mother of a god's children, I must be important enough to be loved and remembered, to finally be worth that. I must be, like I wasn't when I was a girl.

Suspended, lost in water. Staring at the surface, the refracted clouds and sun above. I wanted to die and live at once, to die out of this old, tired, wasted life.

The world rushed by, a blur of gray sky and golden trees and brown-black road. Eventually, we came to a whiter, bluer world and ran alongside a wide river. It must've been deep, I thought. Deep enough to drown in.

"What river is that?" I asked, pointing.

You said, "Providence. It and the Seekonk River bleed into each other."

The river rolled on and on. "And they all bleed into the ocean."

"Yes. There's a little cave where the ocean has hollowed one out, Violetwalk Cove. Maybe we can visit there."

The drive was long, but eventually you parked by the side of the road, and we strode down an incline until the dull grass became sand. I'd walked on sand left from the creeks at home when they swelled with rain and then receded, but something about this crunch, even without touching it, felt different. The brown loafers you offered me were a little worn at the heels.

We crossed the white expanse, and I couldn't help thinking we were the only people in the world. I saw some figures in the distance, but no one came near. A faint foulness crept into the wind. I wrinkled my nose.

Your stray hairs, free from your meticulous pins, flowed near your mouth when you noticed my look. "There's a crab breeding ground nearby. That's the stagnant water they stay in."

"Ah." I couldn't help the small sound that escaped me as we slowed and a shimmer caught my eye.

I gazed upon the endless water.

What struck me first about the ocean, god, the smell, color, noise—I couldn't make them all out. I stared and stared and stared. Oftentimes at home, especially once I became pregnant, my senses became more acute, exhausting my mind. I'd struggle to talk or sort them all out. My hands would tremble, and Papa would shake me, making them tremble more.

I was struck by the glorious jewel color of the sea. Neither truly green or blue. Smooth and rough at once as it seethed white only a foot from our toes.

The vast Atlantic, its promises of secrets and whale songs. Loud, quiet; frenzied, sage.

You pointed to the far right. "See there, the masts? There are a dozen old ships, all wrecked upon each other."

No wonder Papa's books say the gods that are not in the vast cosmos beyond sleep in the water deep below. What religion, once people saw this mercury expanse of the unknown, wouldn't think it was divine? No wonder the poems you kept treated beauty and terror as one.

> *Roll on, thou deep and dark blue Ocean—roll!*
> *Ten thousand fleets sweep over thee in vain;*

My chest hurt, but I didn't want to exhale, blink, lose the moment, the fatigue and arousal. Heat stirred in my throat and below my navel. How easy it truly must've been for sailors to be compelled to toss themselves over the ship, under the shadowed brow of their masts.

> *A shadow of man's ravage, save his own,*
> *When for a moment, like a drop of rain,*
> *He sinks into thy depths with bubbling groan,*
> *Without a grave, unknelled, uncoffined, and unknown.*

Once we are all gone, our bones dust in the sand, this is what will remain, tapering over the beaches like a triumphant shroud.

As the sun set, part of the water bloodied, red as wine.

"What does it make you feel?" I asked you breathlessly, needing that reference, that stable part of the drawing compass.

"Nothing," you said.

I blinked. When my trance broke, the profile of your face was flat, inscrutable, as you looked at the waves. "Really?"

"Yes," you answered evenly, "it feels like that." While the ocean was untamed, you spent so much time killing parts of yourself. "Like going to sleep after opium."

Sometimes there were emotions too overwhelming, too much of

everything, that they felt like nothing. In this universe, I've learned nothing isn't an absence. The void hungers.

"Homesickness," you whispered, eyes drooping, the tide whorling in them, and I wasn't sure what you meant.

I stared at you, and my eyes grew heavy and stung. "I wonder what Wilbur'd think of this. Or his..."

You broke your stare at the ocean to gaze at me.

"He's my son." I told you. "He was. Is." My stomach lurched. Couldn't take that knowledge back.

"Ah." By your side, you rubbed your forefinger against your thumb. You wore white gloves. My eyes flickered to your neck, lingering on your scars peeking out of your collar. They were far from the strangest thing I'd seen. The only thing that was odd to me was that these marks occupied both sides of your neck like deliberate scars, but I kept my peace.

Your jaw worked. "This makes me want a smoke," you said. Your fingers stopped fidgeting and curled.

"Oh?" I'd never smoked, so I hadn't understood your mood. As much as you tried to stop, you couldn't help but go to your cigars and pipes for comfort. "Where is the cove you mentioned?"

"Come." You drew so close that I expected you'd grasp my hand, but you didn't. My eyes ached from watching the ocean; it was no longer snowing, but the world was bright. I shivered, but the nights at home had been cold, too, wind whistling through the cracks between thin window panes and wood.

I followed you, staring at the vortex of your black strands pooled at your nape. I noticed some stray fallen hairs on your collar. Your hair frowned in tender curls at the ends, before you lost all of it, but you often kept it pinned and restrained.

We strolled to the far left of the beach. The ocean curved around the sand and, in this moon-slice of East Providence, you showed me a small cavern, lined with jagged, dark rocks. The frigid air made me shiver under my--your--coat.

You shrugged with one shoulder. "A little getaway. Romantic, I suppose, if it weren't so dim and cold." But my attention meandered from the cave as I saw a habit-trail of shining rocks leading into the ocean.

Ghosting away from you, I stepped on one of the rocks, smoothed by wind and water, and then another, which was bigger but dipped down in the bed of sloshing sand and silt. My sole curled against the surface. Water slurried across the rocks, filling the cracks.

You called after me, "Careful. Don't go out too far. The tide'll catch you."

I wasn't afraid. It wasn't as if I hadn't been ensnared by a primordial force before.

"I can swim," I muttered. In the hillsides, I swam in the creek. So, I went out farther from the cove, balancing myself on the arrangement of stones, globs of cooled lava. Here I was, small and cosmic as the wind beat against my outspread arms.

At last, I reached the end and peered down. Lights swam in water; the sky, I was seeing the sky like I had years before. Chaotic but in perfect harmony.

"Lavinia—" I couldn't tell whose voice it was who called me; it was a thousand miles away, twisted into the whorl of wind and seafoam. Instead of breaking the spell, I was drawn further into crystalline oblivion.

The opal of the world, the mouth, the milk of life. I sucked in a breath, and my heart shot to my throat.

Bones on bones upon bones. The biologists said nothing could live at the bottom of the ocean because not even the sun penetrated the depths, but I knew better. No matter how alien or blasphemous to sensitive eyes, life found a way. It was hubris to think that nothing existed where we couldn't tread.

If I could only reach out and grab my husband's clustered body of stars, hold on to what seemed to be a hand, I could get out of this terrible, weak body and be loved as someone. The salt could cleanse me, and the water would rend me. Hold me.

Never forgotten or thrown away again.

"*Lavinia! Lavinia, stop!*"

Before I knew it, my ankles crumpled like wax, and I plunged into the water, which was colder than I thought it'd be. I was completely submerged at first, and though my head surfaced, I floundered in ice-cold light and darkness. I kicked my legs and paddled, but the water gripped me in its vise, and my throat protested when I swallowed its burning salt.

A wave crashed into me, and I found myself in the bright darkness again, eyes wide open, dress twisted around my legs. So seagirt was I, I didn't notice when a grip came from behind and seized me across the chest. I kicked and writhed.

When I understood who it was behind me, I grew limp, and I let myself be pulled to shore. Once we broke the water, you dragged me, a sopping mess, onto the sand, which was coarse and chilly and welcome. My shaking, numb fingers dug into the land, one little white shell scraping my thumb. I inhaled damp cold.

You eased on your hands and knees beside me, our hips brushing against each other, your fingers on mine, skin on mine, glove missing, lost to the sea. A shock passed through me as I coughed and expelled water on the sand.

You peeled the soaked coat off me, and I was too conscious of my dress sticking to my hips and breasts, how it pooled between my thighs. When I was a girl, I never thought of my body as something to hide. If Papa hadn't wrangled me and made me wear coarse linen dresses and undergarments that never quite fit right, I might've played on the hills naked. Danced and reveled in my own personal witches' sabbaths.

Here, I couldn't say I minded the sheerness the water made of my dress. I should've. My body was shameful and bloated ("puffy" was the word I used as a girl), and that was before the conception of Wilbur and his brother. But I liked that the ocean took my humiliation from me.

Your hair had come loose, splayed down your shoulders, flying wild with each raucous gust. The wind was rough against my hair and neck. A shock of goosebumps needled my skin.

Your white shirt was so soaked that I could see your brassiere and skin under it. As freezing as I was, my cheeks grew hot.

You coughed out water, and wiped your mouth with your sleeve, which only made your face wetter.

"W-what happened?" you started, and my throat tensed as, like sea magma, your voice firmed. "Why the hell in Dagon's soggy balls did you—"

"I didn't," I told you, immediately defensive. "I lost balance." Evening mist crept around us, and though they once ceased, more snowflakes fell, melted in your hair and on your high cheekbones.

Voice rough as the ocean's salt, you said, "You could've drowned." To my shock, you weren't angry, ready to smack me.

Guilty, I shook. "I know, but I didn't mean to." Twice you'd saved my life, and that debt weighed on my heart. I half-expected you to leave me on the shore for being too much trouble. "M'sorry, m'sorry."

With you staring at me, wrought, intense eyes bright and full, I couldn't help but notice how lovely you were.

Shutting your eyes, ending the spell, you released a long breath. "Shit." The foaming waves caressed our ankles.

I coughed some more. "I—"

Wearily, you said, bracing a hand against my shoulder, "You're sorry. Are you really?" A note of wryness.

Being so far away and experiencing that twin heart and heartlessness of the ocean made me drunk on awe, reminded me I was alive.

"Yes," I said.

With a huff, your face broke into a grin, the kind when someone's told a ridiculous joke. Hand to your collarbone, you bowed your head and started to laugh madly.

Something broke in both of us, then. For once, that wasn't a terrible thing. We lived in an absurd world, always relenting under its pressure. I let myself laugh, too.

Our peals melted into one another, infecting us both.

You composed yourself first.

"This was certainly exciting," you said, humored. "Thank goodness we both lived. Are you full of any more secrets or surprises?"

Wracking my brain, I said, "I used to draw all the time." I wanted to chide myself for being an idiot.

You pursed your lips. "I have paper I could give you, blank journals I've never used." Just like that, we were past my foolish behavior, even as another wave came and slithered around our legs.

With a shiver, I frowned. "You don't need to..."

You gave me a stiff nod. "I want to."

"I, I shouldn't rely on you." I licked my lips, tasting the brine of the ocean. "I should have my own clothes, my own things, instead of taking from you."

Your mouth moved, but you said nothing.

It was like we saw each other for the first time.

But we were moving ahead, I think. Already, with your short breaths and brows raised in that exasperated shock, we'd broken past some of the bricks.

My fingernails bit into the crook of my elbow. "Sorry."

You raked a hand through your dripping hair. "Please don't apologize."

"It's how I, it's a reflex." I'd chewed my lips bloody with how much I hated how I talked. Always stumbling. Sitting on my knees, hair plastered to my face, I puffed out my chest, my throat burning. "And when you tell me not to do it, I feel ashamed."

You stared for a moment and offered a tentative nod. "All right. I won't tell you what you can and can't say."

I bowed my head. "Thank you. And thank you for saving me."

"You don't need to thank me for that."

"But I want to." When I looked up, I blurted out, "Your eyes remind me of the ocean."

Dryly, you replied, "The thing that almost killed you? I think my eyes are even colder."

I held your gaze, now soft. "I like the color of your eyes better."

"Why?" you asked, as if not believing anyone could love the color of your eyes. I couldn't tell if you were flushed because of my words or my near-death experience.

"It's like grass or strawberry leaves. Or pop bottles."

You said wistfully, "My strange eyes."

And now there came both mist and snow,
  And it grew wondrous cold:
  And ice, mast-high, came floating by,
  As green as emerald.

Like the sea that clutched me tight, while you kept her distance, you were unfathomable. Right here plain in front of my very eyes, but so far away.

Nevertheless, when our eyes met, yours held me as I shivered.

You broke our long, ponderous gaze. "We should go back to the cottage and tuck in before we catch our deaths." Your eyes fell on where I was scratching my arm, where the skin stung, open, my blood mingling with seasalt. Gingerly, you reached out with your bare hand, only lightly grazing my hand, and I stopped scratching.

"You know," you said. "You once asked me who you are to me. When you called yourself an idiot."

I blinked more droplets out of my eyes. "Oh?"

"You're Lavinia, who likes to garden and fall into the ocean."

I offered a small smile. "Thank you."

Your brow scrunched, rivulets of the ocean forming a cartography along your nose and cheekbones.

You ran a hand through your damp hair. "It's getting too dark." For what? I wondered. Now, I know why she feared darkness. "You go first," you said, ready to stand.

The brief snowflakes spiraling down brought on a strange melancholy. As if we were both on the banks between Mnemosyne and the Lethe.

To be stranded there, to have only our cove and cave, I never would've imagined I'd want that. And here I am, debating on whether to remember or forget, knowing there will be another plunge.

"You should go first up to the car," I told you. "It was my fault you jumped in to save me."

"Nonsense. I made my own decision."

The only answer from me was a lament, as my toes tingled with numbness. "I think I lost your shoes."

As we both achingly stood, weighed down by the tumbling ocean behind us, a not unpleasant feeling prickled my heart. A wish to lean into you, to listen to you share poems and stories of your life by the fireplace.

A stupid dream, I told myself. I'd received my first kiss, the kiss of salt, and it did its best to kill me.

7. Azzie

Any symptoms I had before this point were manageable. Then, my hair started to fall out. If I didn't know better, I might've joked it was you falling into the ocean that started it. You shocked the hair off me.

At first, when I brushed it to a flat, black shine, I didn't notice much of a difference. Some strands fell out, but that's the way of things. I'd always been too rough with my hair, stripping it of any waves.

Passing by the stone well, I went to work. Though bustling East Providence was far from the quiet of home, the mornings when fog rolled in from the water were docile. It gets easy for everything to bleed together when you sit in an auto with the edges of the windows misted up with early dew.

I drove past the high, blue Oddfellows' Hall on Warren Avenue, a two-and-a-half story fraternal society built by Gould & Angell, with its Shingle style; often here, cedar roof shakes are dipped in buttermilk during construction to give an aged look. For the first time, I admired the buildings, how much they reminded me of the trading posts of home or Arkham's museums.

Another place I went past was a brownstone building, a restaurant called Lourenço's, where they serve mussels, tiger prawns, and lean steak topped with egg. With my window down, my mouth watered at the mild and sweet odor of seared red snappers. I thought maybe I should take you there one evening.

Truth be told, outside of those places and City Hall, everything else blended together, except for perhaps Little Neck Cemetery, a gated but wooded hillside which had the gravestones of immigrants who traversed the Atlantic on the Plymouth. Whereas much of the town felt artificially old and renovated, the cemetery felt genuinely wizened.

My mind drifted to you, how you weren't here to observe these things with me. You stayed inside often, but when I offered to take you somewhere, your eyes grew round. The cottage was too small to contain your imagination. Your graphite sketches were loose, not scientifically and exhaustively concerned with proportions. Hands became tubed bluebells that droopingly carpeted ancient woods; bodies were curved and fluid, blending into the flowers and trees.

Inside the symmetrical City Hall, for East Providence architecture prided itself on symmetry, motes of dust struck gold. As I pored over zoning documents and put them in the proper order at my desk, the right side of my neck twinged. This was normal, such as when my wisdom teeth erupted. I sometimes felt a pang in the back of my mouth when I ate. Typically, I took laudanum, and as soon as the pain came, it stopped. Nowadays, much less luck.

I inched two fingers under my collar. When I felt the stinging corner of the top scar, the edge that was coming open, I grimaced.

When I pulled my hand away, a spot of blood sank into my glove.

A lump sinking into my stomach, I murmured, "I can't do this." I'm too young. Not ready to feel the pain of my body changing. Even in the auto, I cannot escape; the metal is cold against my fingers.

Damn my body, damn you. For so long, for so much of my goddamn life, my body hasn't been mine. It was stolen from me. Any pleasure, any familiarity, taken. Now, I have it back only to lose control again.

I don't want this, and that counts for nothing.

"Are you all right?" one of the male clerks asked, balancing a stack of papers in his arms. There I was, hunched over with my expression twisted in discomfort.

Hiding my hand behind my back, I offered an obligatory smile. "Yes, sorry. I'm afraid I'm a little under the weather." I feel my neck burning. Shit. I really must put more ointment on my scars.

His eyes twinged in sympathy. "Do you need to leave?" he asked.

"No." I fluttered my hand around the crown of my head. "Headaches, they'll pass with the rain."

Who can I go to for help? Mother is gone.

Mother, Mother never wanted to leave me, so after the beginning of her change occurred when I was a toddler, she returned and stayed. Even if it meant languishing all day in the attic, and I wondered why. Father didn't entertain many visitors, and surely none of the townsfolk would disdain her. Then again, at times Father would have graduate students and faculty from Miskatonic visit, and he often did so unannounced, as he answered to no one, especially not his wife and daughter.

My suspicion is that Father made her stay there, that despite his interests in the worlds beyond the physical, the human, she repulsed him. Yet, things were never so simple with him. Or perhaps with how purposeful he made all his studies seem, I assumed depth in everything. Oh, he couldn't be bad, merely too complex for a frivolous and badly tempered girl like me to fathom.

Nonetheless, it could've been that in isolating her in that one spot, that ever-constant dry attic, she was easier to observe, to unperson, as one pins a beetle between glass slides.

I'm not ashamed of Mother. When she lived in the attic, I never understood why she needed to hide.

But me? I have this life I chose. A home I willingly settled into, a job I pursued, no matter how menial. I want these things; I want to be present in these moments.

No one can know, I promised myself. If I didn't look, I could ignore the changes. They'd fade in time, like my feelings. I could force my body into entropy.

If I didn't look, if I moved on, then I could stop time.

Then. Well. I want to laugh at my stupidity. That was before my ▮▮▮ started to come in and I took to lace collars for everything.

My scalp itched, but I took care not to scratch it while others were looking at me.

I looked at my gloved hands and frowned. More hair on them.

Disgusting. I pressed a hand to my belly. The day before, I started to menstruate, and though they've never been as bad as when I was a girl, the cramps needled the soft space beneath my skirt waistline.

I took off my glove, scratched an insufferable itch on my neck, looked. Like Orpheus, I could never help but look.

Dead skin peeked out of my nails, like the white of an erupting tooth.

I'm becoming like Mother, and I'm not ready. I can never be as strong as her.

But as much as I need to run, I should've run—I can't abandon you, Vin. I know it'll break your heart.

I was supposed to be safe in my cottage, away from Innsmouth and Arkham, never hurt again. Didn't I deserve that? Nonsense. The universe doesn't care what we believe we deserve.

Like everything else, I needed to hide everything. From you. Like when I rubbed your back, and, feeling the electricity, that tension of my skin, your gown. And once you slept, I jolted away and released a gasp, my eyes hurting, my chest and throat tight.

8. VIN

THE NIGHT WE CAME HOME FROM OUR OCEAN VENTURE, AH.
How your wild blackbird hair smelled of the beach when you leaned to
open my auto door. And though we scrubbed ourselves clean, I awoke to
the crust of sand on my covers and between my toes.

For all your usual tidiness and aloofness, watching you, on the shore,
pull off your remaining glove with your teeth did something to me.

Then, it was like nothing happened.

You were about routines, and that brought comfort. I measured the
minutes with the clack of your shoes on the wood and tiles. For once, I
didn't tense when I heard footsteps.

Sometimes, I paced alone in the cottage, unsure of my relationship to
the space, how my body pooled against the sheets in an existence that
wasn't the hills or my town or anywhere near Papa.

And unsure, too, of what I wanted my relationship to be with you.
Since our too-literal trip to the ocean, where surely I made a fool of myself,
something shifted between us, like how a candle first begins to molt.

One evening, you propped yourself in the plush fireside recliner and
murmured verses. Cradling the thin vanilla-colored book, you recited with
a throaty rasp, "*Frankly I wish I were dead / When she left, she wept / a
great deal; she said to me, 'This parting must be / endured, Sappho. I go*

unwillingly'." And: *"And her light / stretches over salt sea / equally and flowerdeep fields. / And the beautiful dew is poured out / and roses bloom and frail / chervil and flowering sweetclover."*

As you looked up by the fire, I held your lingering gaze with those wide green eyes, and you held mine.

Now, thinking over some of the verses, I wonder if this was your way, at first, of testing the tender new understanding between us.

You came and I was longing for you / You cooled a heart that burned with desire.

When you left for work, the books and radio became my world, and they were revolutionary. Papa only kept scientific and esoteric texts, so poetry and fantasy consumed me. And hearing the stories on the radio, the dramas, I was in love. And I realized my floaty way of seeing the world wasn't singular or stupid.

I could indulge my whimsies without judgment. I wore your long white gown without that fear that curdled in my belly when my Papa's eyes fell upon me and his lips curled in self-conscious distaste. The laudanum worked, and I slept until noon.

You returned promptly from work every day. I can't remember all I said one afternoon as we sat across from each other at the dining table. I was talking to you about the radio. "And the music, some of it's close to birds." I meant the jazz, a genre I'd never heard before in my town.

You pointedly stared at the radio. "It's very nice, yes. Though they're not birds."

My reply was clipped, "Of course I know that. They're people. I'm not stupid."

You stared back at me. "I didn't mean to imply that. I only mean it's best not to compare people to animals. But yes, birds are very beautiful."

I prickled, but you were right. It was something I never thought about. "Okay, I see."

When you cracked your neck and set your hands on the table as you shucked off the day, I was taken aback. Your knuckles were pink and chapped. The cold outside must be bad, I thought, if your skin's drying this fast.

I pointed to the cup I set on the counter. "I made some coffee, if it'll help with the chill."

"Ha, thanks." You fidgeted with your hair, pinned back. "I feel like I'm molting."

I observed your hair, and it looked normal to me. Turns out, you were careful to pin it in such a manner that the thinning spots were covered. At the time, you reminded me of one of those long-haired cats who won't have nothing to do with nobody.

I feel guilty over the comparison, after what you said.

Pointing to your knuckles, I stood. "Here. I made a thing with some of the peppermint and aloe you had in the pantry."

You stared, perplexed, as I went into the washroom and took the shot glass off the sink and set it between us. It was the smallest thing I could put the salve, a pale green cream, in; the rest I put in the pantry.

"You made that yourself?" you asked. "I only know very basic recipes." You let me set two of my fingers, sticky with ointment, on your rough knuckles, and I rubbed the pungent, minty salve on your aching skin. My own smelled of sweet almond oil, olive oil, raspberry seeds, and primroses, which I used to protect myself from the sun.

Touching you like this was nice, this small, tenuous amount of trust between us.

What if I kissed your thumb, your knuckles? I struggled with whether I wanted anything intimate to be gentle play, hesitant and slow, or if I wanted you to thrust me into your world and close the biting sea between us with your lips on my thighs, maybe with some teeth.

I teased, "You aren't the only one who knows a thing or two about herbs." I wondered if your father taught you about them, too, but I didn't dare ask.

When you shivered, I froze.

"Don't worry," you said with a short laugh. "It's cold in here." Yes, it was. I finished applying the salve and went back into the washroom to wipe my hands with a towel. When I returned to the table, you observed my work by late afternoon candlelight. It might've been the glow of the little flame, but your expression softened.

As I sat, you said, "That does feel good. Thank you. What made you want to make this?"

I bowed my head and fidgeted my fingers together, unsure how to accept a thanks. "It helps with my joints and blisters sometimes."

Your eyelids lowered, and you hummed. "I see. I think it's done an excellent job."

Absurd thoughts stirred in my mind. What harm would come if, one evening, I asked you to sit with me on the hearthstones, and I slipped that white glove off your delicate fingers, and I let you press your gentle but bold touch to my cheek, my lips?

All the boys in town who ever fancied me did it out of pity or some noble self-deprecation. And I was a disruption. A stone to walk over, not something new in the foundation. I needed to forge my own path, could only follow for so long, but everything was so murky. I'd gone from fate being decided for me to a life entirely new.

I believe it was the next day when you approached me to go out shopping with you.

"Would you like to go buy groceries with me?" you asked me, as I was reading a collection of Keats poems by the fire. You were dressed in a white lace dress and a gray coat, much less scandalous than what you wore when we were at the ocean.

Without hesitation, I said, setting the book on the nearest display table. "Yes."

Your gloved hand was on the crown of your head. The silly thought came to me that I'd like to once again feel your skin. "I was thinking, you're taller than me." For now. "So, the clothes don't quite fit right. Before we get food, we can purchase some new clothes and shoes, just for you. Do you mind walking? We can travel most of the way by auto, but driving through the city can be fraught." And the sun can be taxing, even if the weather's cloudy.

"I don't mind." My years running along hills and pastures kept me used to traveling on foot. I owned no car and couldn't be cooped up in one space for long.

Most of the drive was silent but not tense. I tug my coat tight, and the car smells of pine and rain. I enjoyed sitting with someone and not feeling the urge to go as far as I could.

There was quite a lot of traffic around us, and my chest grew tight. I shouldn't have been surprised, but it was a new experience. I blinked rapidly at the smear of so many lights. Once we got into the city proper, after going in circles, you eventually found a spot to park outside a pharmacy.

"Here," you said, "in the early evening, this is likely the best parking we will find for miles."

When we got out of the vehicle, I gawked. Chimney smoke billowed out of several buildings and found its way on the main roads. I was shocked at how many people were walking on the sidewalks and how many autos were in the streets, so many that they were slowed to a crawl, and people wove between the spaces without a care.

This was nothing like home, and my belly churned. Where I was from, everyone knew everybody else. Here was a wave of strangers in new, fashionable clothes that looked off. Crisp, well-fitted. A sea of black hats. But I was the strange one, used to hand-me-downs from the turn of the century.

The world hit me at once.

An entire stretch before me of old and new.

An antiquated omnibus rolled past us, trotted along by two black horses with white snouts. One of the creatures snorted under its breath. They headed to the bridge that lorded over the Seekonk, which led to Pawtucket. The white engraving on the side of the blue carriage read, *Our Lady of the Sacred Heart*, the name of the closest parochial school.

To our right, two mustached motormen in their black uniforms and bell crown caps stood outside, taking a smoke outside of an open trolley so elaborate it had a striped awning on the outside of it.

As I ambled clumsily beside you, I found my vision blurring all the pointed brown shoes and white boaters as everyone bustled through Crescent Park. You gently put a hand on the inside of my arm to guide me away from the road, closer to a building made of bricks and stonework, mostly painted white.

You led me into a brownstone emporium with rows of more clothes than I'd seen in my entire life. The air is crisp and smells of sweet perfume. Standing near the entrance, you let me roam. The building had a high ceiling with brown walls, the clothes in this section draped over hangers and folded on wooden counters and in peacock rows on the wall.

I gravitated to the blues and purples, at first. Enough of the white clothes. As much as I may look like a ghost to others, I don't like dressing as one. I understand why you preferred the white and gray clothes back then, while I wanted color. You were doing your best to blend in, while I was avoiding the looks of women and their children.

I wonder if, in another life, I would've gone here with my sons. Oh, honey, that tie looks so handsome on your sixty-seventh tentacle.

Pining over the dresses, I ran my hand along the side of one that was a deep blue with golden flowers. Another was purple, and I found I had a fondness for green, the green of my old haunts—the hills, and of course, other things. Among well-made clothes that weren't falling apart and needed to be stitched and re-stitched, it was hard not to feel like a princess.

This wasn't supposed to be my life. I was being too frivolous over pretty things I didn't deserve. Shame flooded me. This was a personal test. Though the comparison didn't come to me then, I suppose it must've been like when the Lady of Shalott left her prison. She was in awe, but she died because the precious things in life were forbidden to her.

Coming over, you ran a hand over your hair. "Get what you want. Get them all." Your expression was soft. When you released your head, some strands flew on the gray carpet, and melancholy crawled across your face.

I hunched my shoulders, a reflex. "Are—are you sure?"

One of your unsmiles came upon your lips. "Absolutely."

After chewing on my nail in deliberation, I chose four dresses, three nightgowns, a dark plum coat, and a pair of brown oxfords.

"Here, I can hold them. It isn't much," you told me, waving before you paid a kindly smiling clerk whose eyes kept drifting to me. It ended up being two large bags, which you picked up with surprising ease. We left.

Half a block down, I caught the scent of butter. Outside the drugstore, I looked inside the window and caught eyes with the soda jerk with his slick hair and red bowtie. Unused to strangers' eyes, I blushed and looked away. When I looked forward or focused on you, it was almost like the lingering stares (*do you see her? do you think that's her real hair color? what's wrong with her?*) from people on the sidewalk didn't exist.

With both hands full, you gestured toward a building with a vertical red sign with a tilt of your head. "Oh, look! The Cimarron. This cinema only opened last year."

We paused outside the building. A strange-looking establishment, I decided, but most of the things here were strange. To me, that wasn't a bad thing. It was different, and I'd take a hundred differents over my terrible, familiar old life. I didn't care how much smoke or litter there was.

I examined the marquee above us. *The Old Dark House* and *Scarlet Dawn*.

"What was the last film you saw here?" I asked, having never seen a film before.

"*Freaks*, back in February. Terribly bizarre story about the carnival."

Carnival. Fuzzy and gray images pranced in my head. "But did you like it?"

"Yes, quite. If you like..." Before you could say more, a man stumbled by us, suit in disarray, hopelessly drunk. His eyes fell on me, and his mouth opened. Before I could move out of the way, he pawed at my hair. The light in his eyes was wild. I stumbled backwards, and setting down the bags, you caught me before I fell. The man gawked, and once I was grounded, you rushed between us.

Despite the bustle around us, I heard what you said to him clearly:

"Friend, if you do that again, you'll find yourself without that hand." Your tone was perfectly cheerful, and with wide eyes, he floundered away, bumping into others. Burrowing my nails into my arms, I wasn't sure what to say, ashamed and grateful, but after we each took a bag, we were already walking away from the theater.

You looked at me, and I nodded, letting you loop your arm around mine.

You navigated me toward the stands with an assortment of trinkets or snacks to offer. Closest to us, popcorn sold for five cents. Cigars for ten. People stare as we pass.

"The auto isn't too far," you said. Like I memorized the curves and valleys of every part of my hills, you knew East Providence.

As we passed, I caught something hanging from one of the stalls. A rope, and despite knowing better, I reached forward and touched it. Coarse, reminded me of—I had the bruises and purple lines on my wrists for months—

I jerked away from your grasp, as if shocked, and stumbled backwards. I accidentally stumbled into someone who veered away from me, staring with a pinched brow.

Between short breaths, I told you, "We, we need to leave."

"All right. It's not too far." You started to go, but then you took notice of my face. "You look a little flushed. I'm sorry. I should've known this would be much to take in." Your eyes darkened. "And that man, that bastard, he should've kept his hands to himself."

I shook my head, lips tight together. A part of me was exhilarated by this new, bustling world. To think I could come out here anytime and feel the same cobblestones as these people, hear the clack of shoes and hooves and smell the smoke of chimneys and autos and trains—it was too much. More than I could've asked for. Living so long in a secluded town, I started to think everything was dying off, that the only living things lurked in dark corners. I barely noticed you relieving me of the bag of clothes.

Deftly, even with the two bags hoisted up, you guided me to a lonely alley between two stores. Abandoned newspapers rippled across the bricks. When we got far enough from any passerbys, you put down the clothes on a dry spot and set a hand on my back, grounding me.

Your forehead dimpled when you realized I wasn't merely out of breath; I was panicked. My chest and throat closed. I thought I'd die. The more I tried to stop breathing rapidly, the more my nerves overflowed.

You murmured, "Shh, it's okay. No one's here but us."

My thoughts kept pouring. Like when I ran. Oh, Wilbur, poor Wilbur. His soft pink-purple eyes formed in my mind, as new as when I held him, slimy with my blood and womb-water.

I sniffed and rubbed my eyes with the back of my hand. A silver eyelash fell on one of my knuckles. "I left him, my son. I left him because I was scared. I was going to die."

"Die?" you repeated. You blinked rapidly, tense.

My voice came out small and uneven. "They were going to burn me on a tree." The white pine atop Blackacre Hill. "Like a witch across the sea." Bound with rope. Trapped again.

Out of the corner of my eye, the shadows of stray cats darted in the alley.

Your eyes flashed. "Who? Who was going to burn you?"

"Papa and the townsfolk. They were gonna do it on All Hallows' Eve for the gate-and-key, an outer god my town worshiped." Who knows what else they would've done before they set me alight?

You grew eerily frozen, eyes dark in thought and recognition. "Gate-and-key, that's—I haven't heard that in years."

The world we lived in became small and big at once. Small because we realized the esoteric secrets hidden in dark forests and pie cabinets, the teeth and gristle stuck to the mortar, weren't things we were alone in knowing. Our monsters weren't ones we fought alone.

Part of me was relieved. Unbidden, tears welled in my eyes. Yes. Not mad. Not alone.

"Your people believed in the Old Ones and Outer Ones," you murmured. I bowed my head, a tacit yes.

More tears leaked down my face. "At home, the gods loved us."

You scoffed. "The gods don't care about us."

Hushed, I protested, "*Don't* say that."

At that, you went quiet and stepped back, but your eyes pierced the ground between us in anger. I held on to the hope that when I died, the gate-and-key would embrace me in silvery tendrils and take me into the moon, take me back as his chosen godswife.

But when the time came to gratefully die...

My words spilled out. "The night, the thirtieth, that night, he, he, Wilbur woke me up and told me what they were going to do. It was like a spell broke. I knew I was nothing, nothing to them, nothing to anyone. I existed for them to kill me like they killed pigs. I'm nothing."

You came close and tenderly squeezed my shoulders. "No, you're not." I couldn't imagine letting anyone else touch me like you did, but I liked feeling your hands on me, comforting me. I spent so much time in my own head, my dreams and nightmares, but you were flesh and blood.

"I should've done it, I think." I was supposed to be the gate-and-key's wife. I wanted that, so why did I run?

To our left, a stray tabby with a missing left ear stared at you, hissed, and ran off.

"Your son woke you up." You must imagine a toddler, looking at me with soft eyes and rosy cheeks. Not a man who, in five short years after his birth, grew as tall as me, became sullen and surly.

I licked my lips. "Y-yeah. He woke me up and helped me sneak out." I knew my home woods well, but not, not anything else. I figured dying if I did something stupid, dying away from there, would be better than what the town had planned for me.

The whip-poor-wills' song, mocking me, telling me I'd fail because I was an idiot inbred hick in a place the world shunned. Stupid, bad teeth, weak chin. I was so worthless people in that shit town didn't want anything to do with me, too white trash for white trash.

I finished, "And I left him. I left them there with Papa. And them."

You said softly, "I'm sure he understands." To my shock, you raised your palms to rest on my cheeks, caressing my tears away with your thumb.

"I left him and his brother." They weren't right. They weren't right like other babies. Wilbur, and his brother, who only had half a human face. Half a face, with my hair and one violet eye, but then hundreds of other eyes all over his body. Some white, some blue, some yellow. Some that were colors that made my head hurt when I tried to see and identify them. "We only had each other in the world. And I left."

I hated myself for thinking of my sons as abnormal. That was as bad as outright calling them monsters. I loved them. They were my sons; they came from me. If they're monsters, abominations, so am I.

Wilbur, his hand wrapping around my thumb, the way he'd sleep with his fist in his mouth, the four months he was a baby before he started to grow in ways that shocked me.

Sliding my back against the bricks, and sitting, I whispered, "And I left them, left them. They were me, they were all I was good for." I knelt with my arms draped over my knees.

You crouched on the alley stones with me. "You shouldn't think of them at all." Terrible advice, but it worked for you. So you thought. "You should focus on your healing, and if even a single thought of them prevents that, leave it."

Your collar was lower, and I caught the inflamed skin around your neck scars. Something moved under there besides muscles, air, and blood. Soon, our days of dancing around each other would come to an end.

"I, I..." I couldn't think of how to word my feelings. You waited, and even when my problems weren't absolved, I felt like if you couldn't fully understand how I coped, then you understood my loss, my distance from home. I often felt self-conscious about what I could ever do for you to return your kindness, and I would soon find out.

"Here." You were at a loss, uncomfortable. "Why don't I get you some ice cream?" When I didn't immediately answer, you added sheepishly, "Unless you want to go home. That's good with me, too." Home.

"Sure," I muttered. "Ice cream sounds nice."

You scratched at your neck. "I like the coffee flavor. What do you like?"

I thought about it. "Strawberry."

"Good, good. We can do that." When you stood, you reached out a hand, and I took it.

I offered a soft smile. "It's awfully wicked cold for ice cream, isn't it?"

You blinked, flustered. You were cute like that, your grip still gentle on mine. "I, well. Perhaps hot chocolate."

"Does the theater still have showings? I've never seen a show before."

Light dawned in your eyes. "Let's go see."

9. AZZIE

IN THE LIVING ROOM LAST NIGHT, I CLUTCHED THE CURTAINS and eyed them in disgust. Despite my best efforts, they've been mildewing again. Worse, my fingers leave behind traces of a clear ooze.

When you told me about your sons, that your town worshiped an Outer God, the gate-and-key, I shouldn't have been surprised. How short-sighted of me to think the occult fascinations of my town were solitary to that one place. I suppose I thought the ocean dazzled my people, kissed only us with its secrets.

Children. You were a mother. Are a mother. I've never considered having children. Given the extraordinary circumstances of those twelve years I cannot speak or write about, especially the latter few years, I can't say marrying a man again has been in my sights.

So, suffice to say, I was ignorant of your plight. I still am.

Nevertheless, I had some ideas, and I was goddamned furious, but I knew my anger would upset you.

I hated leaving you alone when I worked. You didn't need to be by yourself, especially because you said you thought that you were nothing, and in your grief over home and your son; I didn't fear the cowards who threatened you; I feared you'd kill yourself, blaming yourself for the hatred forced upon you by those who never deserved to know you, ever.

So many questions pooled in my mind about you, as you sat in the recliner that next morning and stared glumly at the window, thumbing the ticket stub. Dr. Phillips assumed you had a husband, and I thought nothing of it. Papa and the townsfolk, you said. In that town, you only had yourself, and perhaps your sons.

We only had each other in the world.

A headache crept into my skull, the sloggy, wet kind that pools from behind the eye to the back of the neck. I decided to leave work early. The drive was slow as rain torrented down in one minute and then ceased in another.

When I arrived home, I heard the crackling radio before I opened the door. As I entered, you sat by it with your head dreamily on your crossed arms. A science fiction drama about aliens, from what I gathered. You turned it down a little.

When you raised your head, I saw a smeared graphite doodle of a goat-monster.

"How did you sleep?" I asked you.

"Well." A pause. "You're early."

"A slow day. Ran out of papers to sort." My compulsion was to lie rather than admit an emotional truth: I was worried about you.

You didn't buy it. At least, that was my interpretation of your side glance.

"I thought we might eat," you said. Muffled static.

I waved a hand. "Go on. I neglected to see how the strawberries are faring."

"I made a plate for you," you told me.

I was touched by that, and I caught myself staring at your lips; as soon as I was eleven years old, something stirred in me when I'd catch a look at a pretty woman's lips or nicely shaped legs. And how do I say it? I've always liked how your lips look, though I doubt that'd sound romantic aloud. I'm not even sure what would sound romantic.

You'd baked and seasoned chicken. It was more effort than I often managed. Most days I couldn't tell anyone about the aches in my knees and hips, the fatigue. I was too young to feel such things, they'd say. Wait until I'm fifty to complain about real pain.

When I ate, despite my awful headache, I realized I was famished.

"This is excellent," I said between bites.

Your cheeks grew red, but your expression was coyly humble. "Yes, well. I did all the cooking at home. It isn't much." Your papa made you do so much, molded you into a second wife like some men try to make women their second mothers, but you weren't allowed to take credit for anything.

Setting down the plate, I said, "Oh, don't be modest." I looked up and decided to tease you. "Your face is red. I thought your burns were healing." It was in good humor, but you withdrew, and I relented. "For..." Forgive me, I wanted to say. That was a concession. No, I couldn't say it, some idiot pride in me.

Your violet sleeves were rolled up, and I saw your scars where you'd worry your nails into your skin. It hurts me to think you do that to yourself because of the actions of your bastard father and the bastard townsfolk. If I could throw them all into a pyre, I would.

I couldn't help myself, pointing to my own wrist. "The marks on the inside of your elbow. You scratch yourself." Your lips are beautiful, and yet they're often bloody and torn. I couldn't, I can't forbid you from acting on these compulsions. So often, I'd dig my nails into the base of my skull, the tender part of my scalp. It grounded me. I could only offer alternatives as a distraction.

You shrugged. "It's not really that I mean to. It just happens."

I stood and took the plate to sink. "Here, let me show you something." I went to my bedroom, and you sat patiently by the desk with the radio.

I carried my typewriter to you, setting it on the desk. To let anyone so much as look at my typewriter was sacred, like how people in my town, when they would marry, would twine their fingers in bowls full of sea salt and blood taken from the crooks of their elbows. Later, I let you taste the wine of poetry with my books, you loved the taste of verse.

"If you want," I told you, "you can write with this." *May I write words more naked than flesh, / stronger than bone, more resilient than / sinew, sensitive than nerve.*

"Write what?" you asked, eyes wide. Though I often needed to look up at you, you looked up to me.

"Anything," I said. "I used to type up some poetry here and there.

Imitations. Don't ask for requests. I'm dreadful at making anything beautiful." You looked up at me in astonishment. "I know what you're thinking. I don't seem like the artistic sort."

"That's not true," you said with surprising passion, one thumb glimpsing the A key. "Your garden is art."

I took that in. "I suppose. Hell, when I was in university, I didn't study art."

"What did you study?" you asked me.

"Medieval metaphysics."

You hummed to herself. "Of course. Time and space."

"Yes, the nature of the cosmos and such. I was the only woman at Miskatonic."

"I can't imagine." You paused, eyes going back and forth, mulling over your next words. "Not once did Papa discuss university. Most people got married and worked on their land. Or fixed things."

"It's not too late," I say, "to go."

You bit your lip. "I'm not sure I'd want to be in a place like that, learning the things my papa knew." If only I didn't understand. As a child, I spent so long curious about what Father knew that I didn't realize I needed to spend time on my own knowledge. My own secrets.

I said, "You could study whatever you like, and it doesn't have to be at Miskatonic."

You hummed, fingers drifting over the keys. I left you to tap away, make your own, better worlds.

Night came colder than the one before, frost creeping along the windows. As I prepared for bed and brushed my hair, a clump fell right in the palm of my hand. Not a rats' nest. A wad that slipped off my scalp, never to return.

The horror came slowly, froze me into a temporary death. Swallowing down my gasps ached, and chills radiated down my arms.

"Shit. Shit." My words were quiet and stunted.

My gums started to ache, and an image flashed in my mind. Looking up, far up, and seeing Mother like this, bent over the sink, eyes slick and a sickly color, like olives. Mucus and blood formed a trail down the drain. As scary as it was then, it felt distant.

This feels like a punishment. Whether what happened in my past damned me, whether it was even my fault, this is a consequence. If only I did something different, if only I'd gotten away from Father and his study that smelled of parchment and dust, I could've avoided this fate. Even if it's my Mother's blood that burgeoned this change in me.

Must find a way to blame myself, always. Because at least that means I have some semblance of control to change things. I'm not really a pawn waiting to be toppled.

I can't do this, I thought yet again. Couldn't let you see me weak, see me cry.

I'm supposed to be strong. I can't do this I can't do this I can't do this I can't I ca I ca I ca

Hair grows back.

Hair grows back.

10. VIN

DESPITE BEING IN THE PRETTY GREEN DRESS YOU BOUGHT ME, I helped you care for the garden. We had baskets and picked the last of the strawberries in peace. Some were still on the cusp of ripening. I realized faintly it'd been a few days since I'd bitten my lip bloody.

You adjusted your black flat cap. "They go dormant in the winter, so I want to sell as many as I can." I wasn't sure how to tell you how good the hat looked on you. You gave me one, too, in case the sun emerged from the clouds. Every day was an expanse of gray and white, frost clawing its way onto the corners of the cottage windows. We kept the stove on, more often than not.

"Have you ever made anything with them?" I asked you.

Plucking another berry into your basket by me, you replied lightly, "As you've seen, my cooking skills are very basic compared to yours. You saw that burned johnnycake."

"Yes, unfortunately," I joked.

Looking at the bushes, you scratched at your neck under your collar. "What would I even use them for, a topping on a pie?"

"That sounds good. I always did like making strawberry and black-berry cobblers."

You nodded, eyes distant. A soft wind, the promise of rain. "I suppose...I suppose it's something to do. But I warn you, my cooking doesn't extend much past fish and rice. And burned johnnycake." You could be so self-effacing.

"Let's do it. Let's make one soon." I don't know what brought on my chipper nature that day.

You tasted one of the strawberries, solemn. It seemed we operated on a pendulum where one of us would be dour or sullen and the other would work to lighten the mood.

Some of the juice dripped down your chin. Before it stained your white shirt, I wiped it off with a finger. You didn't flinch away or go eerily still, only watched me as, putting my finger to my mouth, I sucked on it. A little sour in the sweetness, the crack of one seed splitting under my teeth.

"Yeah," I said. "Almost ripe." You were staring, and my neck grew hot. "Sorry."

I couldn't read your expression, though I thought I caught the hint of a smile. "No, no. I don't mind. No need to let anything go to waste." Thunder rumbled in the distance. In my hills, I grew unafraid of it and would dance in the rain.

As we went inside, clothes soaked, you laughed as you shook some of the rain out of your hair. I couldn't shake the feeling of an ominous portent bearing down on our heads.

After we stored the strawberries in jars for the icebox and washed our hands, I found you sitting in the porch rocking chair. As I was in the washroom, I noticed long black strands of hair on the wood planks. You were usually careful about cleaning.

Your eyes were rimmed red. From drink, sleeplessness, or tears, I couldn't tell. You stared ahead in the lengthening pink and purple of dusk above the almost naked trees.

"What's happening to you?" My chest tightened, like it did when I said anything I swore would make Papa turn feral.

"What do you mean?" you asked, snapping from your daze to meet my eyes.

I said, "There's something wrong."

You tried to make your voice light, conversational. "No, there's nothing."

I resented you for that, thinking that you were lying to me because you thought I couldn't deal with whatever you told me, that I'd crumble from the truth. I was being too defensive based on what I'd been through, so used to people telling me the world wasn't as I saw it. If I told Papa the sky was blue, he'd say it was orange, that I was seeing wrong. That I was stupid.

Truly, you were lying to yourself and hoping to have the outside world conform to your needs.

I shook my head. "Don't lie to me. Not you. Everyone thinks I'm stupid. An idiot."

You frowned, and shadows welled like bruises under your eyes. "I don't."

"Then why're you lying to me?" I was flustered, but I kept on. "I've seen that you're losing your hair. I've swept it up."

Your jaw tightened. "It's my business, not yours." At the end of the day, this was your choice over what was happening with your body. If you didn't want to tell me, you didn't need to.

I crossed my arms over myself. "Fine. You don't need to say what it is. M'sorry."

You sighed and rubbed the space between your brows. "No, don't be."

"I want to help," I said, kneeling by the chair. It might've been irrational to feel guilt over a physical struggle neither of us could control, but I did, and I wanted to do something, anything. A habit.

You looked sadly at me. "Nothing can help this."

"How do you know? Do you need Dr. Phillips?"

Your hand clenched the armrest. "No. What happens to my body is my business. Not his, not anyone's. Mine."

With that, I didn't press the matter. "Okay, okay." As much as I wanted to say you being sick *was* a doctor's business, I know what it's like having no control over who gets to inspect your body.

The skin around your eyes scrunched. Something like regret.

You frustrated me with how you martyred yourself, didn't trust me to care for you. Then again, it wasn't personal, was what you would say, and it was true.

You reminded me most of Wilbur, who'd never let me tend to any of his scrapes or splinters. He'd frown and shake his head as he yanked splintered wood chips out of his knees. That was the one thing in you that reminded me of him.

All the same, you could be wonderfully dramatic, as if I could talk. In trying to keep yourself from being stabbed, you were letting the knife lodge itself deeper into you. Like when Papa sliced me open—I had so little power, so frightened. Every boundary, every little interest he told me was insipid and every space I tried to claim as mine, even my own body.

But it was familiar.

Before I could suck the miserable affection back inside, I said, "Oh, Azzie."

Your lips parted. "Azzie." You touched a finger to your chin in thought. "No one's given me a nickname like that before."

The conversation died like the darkening sun after that, and we lapsed into a liminal pause, though I caught the remorse in your eyes as you broke our shared gaze.

It looked too much like longing.

11. AZZIE

THREW UP BREAKFAST. BUT ATE A LITTLE JOHNNYCAKE, CRISP around the edges, and seem to be fine.

Gums hurt, gills aren't having it anymore. They'll open one way or another.

Drank a little water, seems to be okay. Office told me to take the time I need. I must sound miserable.

Vin, you were right to be offended by my lies and secrecy. How frustrated I must make you, so fickle and distrustful all the time. A thousand times, someone could be honest with me, and I'd try to catch the one time they lie and "betray" me.

You broke down, confided in me, and I didn't have the strength to do the same with you. I wasn't ready. I don't know if I'm ready now. Such horrible things aren't worth reminiscing on. You're so much more than what you've endured, what others, in their weakness, said or did to your body. We exist separate from that, on another plane.

Often, I feel my body detached from the rest of the world, drifting away from everything else, including me.

I fear if I linger on that too long, my soul will leave, too. The dreams where my soul stares above my body, slipping out of my mouth and into the ether, they make me wake in a cold sweat with vomit in my throat. That's why I have the laudanum.

My body exists on a lonely plane. And then I dig my nails into my scalp, and I remember that even if I live in the world where I was hurt and a pawn of Father's whims, I don't accept that. I escaped.

I thought I did.

I've been secretive, and you tend to me as the days grow harder. I'm afraid I cannot hide forever, and I'm sorry.

You paid attention to everything; you needed to keep watch to survive. I didn't know how you learned the doctor's name. I didn't know I'd become more careless in hiding my evolving illness.

Can't say much more, must sleep, but I want to. I must. Sleep feels like a sin when I'm on borrowed time. When we, we. No. We've agreed. Tacitly. In words, indirect or no. I'll transition here, even if it's slow. Even if the water here is nothing compared to the ocean, saltless and thin.

The ocean. Mother told me it was beautiful in ways she couldn't describe, where the cities deep down have jewels and metals that make gold look dim. She would share poems she thought were majestic while I found them terrifying. Lines such as these:

> *The many men, so beautiful!*
> *And they all dead did lie:*
> *And a thousand thousand slimy things*
> *Lived on; and so did I.*

In the end, I suspect that she joined those thousand thousand slimy things.

Even if Mother's still at the house, I can't face her with all that's happened. I can no longer pretend to be that precocious girl she loved with the caress of a damp fin on my cheek.

What would I say to you, if I were to never see you again, Vin?

My only company, and yet I haven't confided in you like you have to me, there in the woods by the white mushrooms, orange fungus, and green pond. Where you revealed what your papa did to you on a stormy May evening.

12. VIN

THE AFTERNOON WAS FROSTY WHEN I FOLLOWED YOU INTO the woods to a small waterfall not far from the back of the cottage.

Before we went, I took a broom and swept away your fallen hair and mourned it with you, and I mourned how miserable you must be.

When I saw a crow try to inch toward the garden, its shiny feathers reminded me of your curls. You snapped your teeth at it with a low croak erupting from deep in your throat, and it flew away with an indignant caw.

Outside, you drank a coffee cabinet from one of your vodka glasses. You did it like you usually ate and drank anything: slowly, as if afraid of accidentally swallowing glass. I stared far too long.

I've struggled to discern the difference between jealousy and desire. When I admired your eyes, so green I can only compare them to the meadows deep in the hills, did I resent them? And if I felt resentment toward your eyes, was it because I wanted eyes like yours or because I could never admit to you how much I loved them and drowned in them?

In the clearing, a waterfall of about fifteen feet rushed into a small collection of green water, tumbled over rocks and fallen tree branches, and headed downstream. Because of the recent rain, the pool sought to overwhelm the banks.

When you went swimming in your shirt and slacks, I said nothing and only watched as you eased into the water, not commenting on the cold. I'd thought someone as professional as you wouldn't like sinking into the water and muck and silt, but like you dove into the ocean without hesitation, you easily knifed a white trail of bubbles through the water, unfazed by what direction it went. On my tongue sat the taste of the syllabub you brought with us, a fine mix of sweet cream, milk, wine, and strawberries. Amid birdsong and the laughter of the water, I grew a little dizzy.

"Don't tell anyone," you had said mischievously. "Wouldn't want to have the contraband taken." The alcohol loosened my lungs. No longer did I have that heaviness, that tether that kept me docile.

You rejoined me, dripping wet but not shivering, and took a towel I offered. You smelled of earth with a slight flowery scent.

As you twisted the towel in your hair, your movements slow and jerky, we sat cross-legged by each other. The pond water was dark, and nothing was within. No fish, no frogs. Goosebumps prickled my skin, not helped as I perused how your shirt clung to you.

I said to you, "I've been meaning to ask you something, but I was worried how it'd come across."

You set the soaked towel by your other side, eyes on the top of the waterfall. "Go ahead." As if noting my delay, you added, "It takes a great deal to offend me."

"Why do you work?" I inquired. "It seems like you have enough." Especially when you seemed to be having problems with the illness you didn't name, work was a complication. Or it soon would be.

You pursed your lips in thought. "Asenath the simple town clerk. A different skin I never thought I'd wear, but different is good. Better."

Your words resonated with me. A different skin. More like, a different soul. Cleaner, unburdened by fear and grief.

"What did you think when you first saw me?" I asked you.

You hummed to yourself, attention on a yellow warbler in a tree, almost barren with only sparse, orange leaves. "I was worried, confused. Never before have I been that breathless."

"Breathless?" Heat prickled my cheeks. "Why?"

Water fell into your eyes, but you didn't so much as blink as you peered ahead. "It was a shock, finding you." When you rolled your shoulders, I heard one of them pop. "See, I've traveled the East Providence woods many times. When I came here, I wanted to be gossamer in the wind, translucent. Temporary." You stroked damp hair behind your ear, and I noticed your top neck scar was pink with irritation. "I fluttered past everything without seeing or leaving a mark. But then I saw you, and you were real. And I couldn't just flutter by."

I crossed my arms over myself. "Do you feel like things are different, that you're leaving a mark?"

You paused in thought. "I don't know. I'd like to think so. Everything in this world is so temporary. In the eyes of the gods, we're only transients hitchhiking from one reality to another." You shifted, so I couldn't see your eyes. "Pawns."

This world, the Dreamlands. "If only you knew. If only I…" I swallowed thickly and ran a finger along the petals of a dead dandelion. "I had a dream about my sons last night."

"Did you?" Though I couldn't see your expression, I imagined it was impenetrable.

The water lulled me, and I found myself rocking back and forth. "They weren't like nothing I'd ever seen. They weren't all human. My papa…"

I froze. The world became the tip of a pin as I returned home. The barn behind our home, which was bigger than the house I used to crawl up in the loft and have wild dreams of playing with the cows in the stars. Nightmares danced there, nightmares with no faces and mouths for hands.

You were getting sick in front of my eyes, and here I was, thinking of retreating further into my head.

I dug my nails into the crook of my arms. "I want to tell you what it was like. I need at least one person in this world to understand, in case anything happens to me." My eyes stung, and I slapped my hand over my mouth.

"Nothing's going to happen to you, Vin," you soothed. For too long, I was told I was going to die, and the whip-poor-wills would claim my soul. The fate of everyone who lived at home. How could I avoid fate? The only way I could think of was living among the stars; birds couldn't fly there. "You can tell me anything."

A long quiet. The details of what I went through were embarrassing, shameful, made people uncomfortable. Not the topic of good and polite conversation.

The alcohol made the boundaries I set for my thoughts softer. Shit, it was uncomfortable for everyone else, but how did they think it made me feel to live with it? I was expected to keep silent and suffer, so others could thrive. And I'd watch them from my lonely shithole.

My fingers brushed the lifeless stem of the dandelion. "It was sometime in May, six years ago. Hadn't stopped raining for weeks." My throat constricted, and I pinched the dandelion too hard, so it snapped in two. "Papa came and got me out of bed and dragged me to the barn behind the house. It had this rusty smell, like metal, but with a little blood."

You watched me now, saying nothing as I continued, "He tied me to the table, and he read out of a book, he took—he took one of our only goats, Missy." Who I nursed since she was a baby. "And sliced her throat." The blood poured in the circle he'd made with chalk, and then dribbled. "I was trapped there on the table, my legs spread open with rope."

I bumped my wrists together and parted them, making a motion like I was swimming frog-style. Your breathing went uneven. "And he made me recite the words from an ancient book with a strange, old smell." The leather was lighter than his other tomes, in some spots; it looked like a patchwork of different fabrics. Some of his books smelled foul, the edges rotting green and bruise-blue in a different manner than that telltale film of mildew. "I wish I passed out after...the gate-and-key, the god Papa wanted to give me children, the god was *inside* him; I thought it'd burned his soul out of his body when he, when it was on top of me."

Your arms beaded with moisture, you kept rubbing your mouth with your palm. I didn't know what that meant. Your other hand gripped the empty drink glass like a vise. Your knuckles were sickly white.

It was hard to keep my head straight, not to bow. "And then, after that, even after my belly grew, things went on the same. I was always tired, but I cooked like I was supposed to, I washed laundry, and Papa and I ate at the same table, as if nothing happened." Except, as much as I wish I could say I hated him, it was hard as lonely as I was for thirty-some years. But my emotions when I was around him darkened, those softer moments he showed to me prickling my heart. Instead of always obeying, he irritated me, so I withdrew into myself. If I was going to die, what was one cross word or some sulking?

I thumbed the fabric above my belly; my navel ached with remembrance. I remember a hot cloth on my brow, the bittersweet mix of laudanum and crushed willow bark on my tongue. Papa coaxed a hand down my shoulder, and I shivered with fever.

A sharp, terrible sound pierced the air, a shuddering crack. My vision shuddered purple.

I snapped back to reality, my toes dipping into the water. I looked at you, hoping you wouldn't be disgusted with me. You stared into space with intensity, not looking at me. My heart clenched because I figured you must've seen me for what I was, what people called me: an inbred freak. A creature who birthed monsters from occult incest. A hideous slut. My eyes snapped to your lap, your tight grip on the syllabub glass.

Then, with a loud, high crack like the split of god-thunder, you crushed it in your hand, not so much as flinching when the shards splintered and buried themselves in your skin.

At the time, I didn't know how you could ever manage to break a glass with one bare hand. Some of the shards spat out on the grass, while others flitted on your legs.

You were bleeding. Instinctively, my hands hovered over you. "Azzie!"

You shook your head as you let the glass in your hand, cutting the inside of your palm, fall to the grass with a shake. "It'll heal."

I hesitated when you showed me one of the cuts, shallow but pouring blood. Like alien moss, your skin criss-crossed over itself. It was familiar—Wilbur's skin did that when he got a scrape or cut. The shell that formed was rough and smooth, but with the pebbles of flesh layered over one another like scales.

I gawked, not because this was new, but because I never thought I'd see the unusual healing happen to you.

As you refused my help, we sat in silence again, except for the thundering water, loud as my heart.

But I couldn't take it, couldn't take how the pulse in my throat mimicked the drums of the waterfall. "One day, I found this place where the trees hung low and formed a cross, and I huddled under them as it began to rain. It didn't keep me from getting wet, but it helped, and I fell asleep. I was eight months pregnant by then. Every day, I was exhausted. When I woke up, Father stood over me, curled up in the dirt and mud."

My voice broke. "I hated him." A simple word for it, something that brought my guilt. He was my papa; I should've loved him better. Yet he never thought about loving me more. "The woods and hills were *my* places to roam, and I remembered that anywhere I went, he knew better. He could always find me. Nothing was ever mine that wasn't also his. There wasn't a single shadow in any grove he didn't know. That's when I realized I needed to run, but I didn't. I let him carry me back, and I stayed for about five more years. Five too long."

Somberly, you said, "It's not as easy as we think to leave." A pause, and you met my eyes. A fire stormed in them. It exhilarated me. "That won't happen to you again."

"You can't promise that." We were only two lonely girls, nothing girls, and the universe was vast and omnipotent. "Papa, my sons..."

"Your father was a monster, and so were they." You, forward-thinking Azzie, always ready to paint the past and everything in it in one red brush. And move on once you made everything easy and simple to digest or dismiss.

You couldn't understand how I clung to my sons, especially Wilbur, fondly when they'd been conceived like they were. If Papa and the gate-and-key weren't innocent, my sons must've also been instruments in my misery. So, you hated them, too, for traumatizing me and "holding me back."

I couldn't let what you said be. "He was, but they weren't."

You shook your head. "Yes, they were. Creatures from beyond don't love like we do. They don't care about love or family or anything beyond what entertains or fascinates them. And some don't even care about that."

My hands curled at my sides. "How do you know? Would you say the same about whatever you're becoming?"

That stoked the fire. You snapped, "I'm not becoming anything."

I stood abruptly, towering over you. "Your *hand*. You must really think I'm a dumb hick. Just because I never went to school doesn't mean that I never read, that I don't *see*."

Uncertainty flickered in your face as you bolted up, glass shards showering off you. "I know that. Of course I know that." You took a step forward, and the boots you'd put on after your swim crunched.

Furiously, I continued, "Do you? Besides, no matter what elsewhere the gate-and-key comes from, they were my sons. *I* had them." Even if Papa was there during the birth, if Mamie Bishop served as midwife and swore herself to secrecy, I was alone as my body convulsed and released blood and amniotic fluid and starry green ooze on the hay Miss Mamie Bishop lightly covered with a blanket. "My sons are half me. No matter what my papa or a god did, I carried them. If they're monsters, so am I. Remember that."

You lurched backwards, as if I'd staggered you into a corner. "No, you're not a monster."

The space above my elbow twinged from clenching it. When I unfolded my arms, I saw I'd drawn blood. You released a shuddering breath, taking one of my hands in yours and grazing your thumb over my knuckles. You looked down and shut your eyes, inhaling deeply.

Softly, I told you, "I'd never call you a monster, nor your mother. I'd hope you'd give me the same consideration."

"My mother?" you asked, and when you saw my look, your face was grim; the people of Innsmouth only let their men take Deep One "brides," despite the beings having no set sex or gender.

You are the progeny of a bloodline of Deep Ones while I, startouched, started a bloodline. The bigger babe, he never meant to hurt me; he couldn't help how long his teeth were. But Wilbur, he gave me strawberry tarts and cobblers. He worked around the house, scrubbing away dust and sweeping dirt away, so I didn't need to like Papa said I did.

You squeezed my hand, the coarseness of your newly healed scars scraping against my skin. A jolt of lightning surged up my arms. "You shouldn't feel like you have to be their mother. Or his daughter. Or that thing's wife. Those things, they aren't real like we are. The Deep Ones are flesh and blood. Even entities like shoggoths are aliens enslaved, their identities stolen from them, they bleed. But still, the people in my town deluded themselves into thinking the gods cared about them. My father believed in all that nonsense, and it propelled his studies."

"What happened to your father?"

With a huff, you dropped your hand from mine and met my eyes. "He's dead, and good riddance." We stared at each other for a good while, the air swollen and thick around us. "Like I've said, the gods don't care about us, and neither do their spawn. They use us until we die or become mad."

Your throat twitches when you swallow.

I said softly, "If your people are Deep Ones, I'll lose you."

Darkness flickered in your eyes. "I've already offended you. It doesn't seem like it'd be a loss."

"It would. It'd be another one." I chewed on my lip. "I let him..." I let my next words fade. For the long time I lived with Papa, I let him slowly burrow his thoughts and feelings about me into my skin, let him drain me. I was consumed by the unfairness of it all; I never asked to be his daughter.

But no, it wasn't so simple, that silly Lavinia only needed to escape to be free of his insidious influence. Even miles away in another state, his words creeped into my thoughts. Less frequent now.

You said fiercely, "You didn't let him do anything. You didn't do anything wrong."

My voice was bloated and small at once, mucus in my throat. "Sometimes I think what he did to me is all I am." And because of how he hurt me, I thought I'd forever need to remember it and live all my life either with the rape as a reference point or an inevitability.

With conviction, you said, "You're an artist, a reader. You love flowers and the ocean, though you've seen it once and almost died right in front of me. You're my..." A hefty silence as more water fell from your hair. "If I had your father right here, right now, he'd wish a bloody ritual was all I'd want him for."

I blinked rapidly. "Please don't."

You heaved a sigh and lowered your shoulders. Your jaw continued to work.

As we looked at each other, my gaze moved to your shoulder. I had to look down, and softly, you smiled, an invitation, and I leaned my forehead against the fabric of your damp shirt. My chest ached.

"What was your second son's name?" you whispered, sliding one hand along the middle of my back.

"Hm?"

"One of your twins' was named Wilbur, but the other, you've never said."

"Horror," I replied. "He took more after his father." I sniffed. What a horrible thing. To call a baby "Horror." A baby, my baby with half my face.

You kept your voice calm, but a tremor came from your throat, your quickening pulse against my brow. "Did you ever tell anyone what he did?"

"No. The townsfolk knew I was pregnant, but they hated me for it. Called me names. Well. More names." I felt bad for bringing this up. Between the two of us, I wasn't the one losing my hair. You were the one suffering now, not me.

I never asked for that May Eve, when you hear the people chanting in the woods and the dogs howling, to happen. Didn't ask for what happened to be called rape. Didn't ask to be raped, to be the fallen woman who endured shaking heads and sneers and piteous stares. A floozy, a slut, they called me. The unmarried woman who slept with an unknown man or, worse, her own father. Never covering my feet, always wandering in daydreams of goat-women and flute players in a rose-gold dream-city, not caring if my dress rode up. Practically asking for a tragedy. Insane Whateley's daughter, and Wilbur became idiot Lavinny's brat.

If I admitted my sons hurt me and traumatized me when they came into existence, I was bad. Not a good, sweet mother. If I admitted I loved them, these alien spawns, I was bad, cowed by my abuse.

You scoffed and held me even closer. "What a load of bullshit. Blamed you? I don't blame you for anything. To go through that alone, shit, Vinny, I'm so sorry."

You were right. What a load of bullshit.

When I slipped away, your smile was sad. "Oh, Vin, you shouldn't put so much trust in me."

I wasn't sure where that came from. "I don't trust many."

You replied, "I can't say I blame you."

Earnestly, I said, so close our noses almost brushed against each other, "But I do trust you."

Your expression contorted, dark lines in the white-yellow wash of your face with the sunlight playing off those captivating eyes. I craved inhaling your rich, spicy salt and tobacco because I feared tomorrow, you'd shut your petals again.

Except, it didn't quite work out like that.

13. Azzie

My health didn't decline all at once. Rather, it bounced. One day, I'd be so animated I'd walk for miles in the forest. The next day or hour, an undercurrent of sickness would thrust me into a cloud of nausea.

You knew what was happening, what these scars were.

Dormant gills. Dormant like the strawberries are in winter; my scars were always these faint lines on the side of my neck, ignored by my hometown because almost everyone had them. In East Providence, I simply hid them.

One evening, I went into the bedroom, with you behind me on the typewriter. I heard you speak; my hair loss was worse, gnarled clumps on the floor.

"You'll need to face this sooner or later," you whispered to my back.

Facing you, I snapped, "You don't think I know that?"

You held your own, standing. "I'm not sure you do."

"That's easy for you to say." My body would make me face myself, one way or another.

Heatedly, you replied, "You don't know how easy or hard it is for me." I was taken back. Living my family curse made it feel like it was a secret dear to me, my own language. You eased back, contemplative. "But after what I went through, I can't be surprised by anything."

"It's different when you haven't seen it." When it's not your skin and hair molting away, sloughed on the tiles and wood like nothing. Me, me in pieces. "It's my body." I ran a hand over my head, but then grimaced as my fingers caught loose hairs, maybe never to return.

Mine, then not.

No, no no no. Hair grows back. Hair grows back.

Hair grows back.

Stupid, stupid Asenath, thinking you could make your own life for yourself.

"Vin, I like my hair." I didn't mean for my voice to be so forlorn.

You frowned and pursed your lips, raising a hand and patting my shoulder.

"What would you do?" I pressed you when you were respectfully silent. "It's easy to say you'll stay now. When I haven't lost all my hair, when I'm not in so much pain I forget how to be happy."

"Do you really think I'm scared of some gills and scales?" You said that, but fear lightning-streaked your eyes. With conviction, you added, "If it gets bad, I'll help you. I'll do anything you need."

It will get bad. "Why?"

You blinked, hand on the bedroom doorknob. "What do you mean?"

A wave of fatigue crashing into me, I sat on the end of the bed and shut my eyes. "Why would you want to be someone's nurse? It'll be quite unpleasant." I'll be unpleasant.

Your eyes and voice softened. "You saved me and gave me a home."

Oh, Vin.

My eyes snapped open. "There weren't any other options. What else would I do, leave you to die?" It was like when you were grateful I saved you from drowning.

"That could've been an option. If I were back in Dunwich, I'd be lucky if they left me to die in the dirt. They were ready to throw me on a pyre. All they saw was some god's toy, my papa's toy. I guess that's because that was all I was, in the end." You came to sit by me.

"No, that's not true." My voice scraped against my throat. "That's not all you are."

"Maybe."

When her fingers brushed against my skin, my wrist, a hangnail lightly digging in, it prickled, but not unpleasantly, and something fluttered in my chest. My throat tightened, and my scars ached.

"I won't leave you," you said. "I know monsters. I've seen them."

I murmured in sympathy, "You've loved them."

An obligation came into you, then. I wondered if you needed to assist me to still think of yourself as worthy of love. Of me.

I knew your trauma. Life for you had been people who fed off you in one way or another until you were violated and abandoned and forced to flee certain death. I wish I could say I didn't understand how that felt.

For so long, for years upon years, I wished to escape my slowly rotting skin, *his* rotting skin. Though I'd never once harmed you as the others had, if I ever leave for the sea to complete my change, I'll be another person, or monster, who left you to your own devices.

After all, you promised not to leave me in the agonizing months to come. What filthy monster would hurt and leave you after that? And I will become filthy, unrecognizable.

"Azzie," you said. "We'll get through this. Somehow." You got flustered, saying that nickname again.

"I like it." You reddened. When I hear my name, my unfortunate name, I only think about how it isn't my own. No birth names are. Father looked at me once and decided, yes, Asenath, you belong to me.

There I was, trembling and worried, and you enveloped me in your arms. Shipwrecked as I felt, it was good to be in your embrace.

I could convince myself that if my body wasn't mine, it was yours.

14. VIN

I WANTED TO SEE WHATEVER THIS WAS TO THE END. IN A world of infinities, I was unsure if there'd be an end, but I was okay with that.

A hard winter froze our pipes—our, my mind was starting to change how I saw space. We managed with good humor.

And an early spring came with little progress with your condition, which made me hopeful for your health. For your ability to stay with me.

You taught me the basics of driving on the wide dirt roads in the wilderness. I was terrible at it, but you were a calm teacher. Once, as my hands trembled on the wheel, you cupped my right hand, and the shaking ceased.

When April came around, I kept busy, less melancholy when I thought about the yellow cakes I made my sons during the festival of the Mother of a Thousand Young, when the girls wore wildflower crowns and lovers would howl and write in the woods. Though we had no cream or icing in Papa's little shack, I'd put strawberries on top of the cakes. Then, I'd wheel Wilbur and his brother around in an old wagon I made. Their mouths and tentacles were sticky with jam and crumbs.

Before they grew too big, and before the wagon rotted with a broken axle.

Azzie: In the blue twilight outside our cottage, even with spring here, the slush outside whitened with a powder of snow.

With you gone, I tindered the fireplace.

Despite the heat inside, goosebumps prickled my arms, like the trees watched me back from outside the frosted windows.

Each morning, I expected to see my sons' violet eyes through the frost, and many days, I didn't look out at all. No, I had my sketches, and then, after you made a trip to the store, watercolors. When I began to grow comfortable, I was ashamed.

I wasn't able to let go of the idea that my trauma was *me*, and I was my own trauma. That meant I'd need to give up on the idea that being a godswife was my horrifying but beautiful destiny.

And I thought if I lost that, I was nothing. That what Papa did, my forced purpose after years of languor and rejection, meant nothing. That the gods didn't care who they fucked and fucked over, that it was really only me, the helpless, nervous spinster the town hated, being brutalized and primed for a violent death, like Mama. And that was it.

For the violence to have been meaningless, I must've been meaningless, too.

Like I grew angry at you for martyring yourself in your own pain, here I was, needing one act of violence to define me. Lavinia Whateley, the victim no one cared about, who was destined to wed an Outer One in the stars. If the gods were apathetic, that meant what happened to me was nothing. My tears. The three days of labor where I oozed blood and slime that oozed like a cracked treacle. My problems with continence after.

Or maybe it was better for me to see my pain as nothing. It was a conundrum, and after years of silence, my ideas of what to do only ranged to extremes. Give myself to the gate-and-key, or give myself to what? The world that despised me or saw me as a curiosity? A freak? The "whore." The "albino."

I did have my comforts. I'd hear you singing at night or as you came home. The words scattered on the porch planks like leaves shaken from your boots. "*Noah stuck the dog's nose in the hole, since all the dog's noses have been wet and cold. It's a long, long time and a very long time, a long, long time and a very long time...*"

Then, the one you sang when you came home from work this one day stuck to me like briars.

"*We'll drop him down with a long, long roll where the sharks will have his body and the Devil'll take his soul.*"

One day, after I heard you, you sighed as you came in. "The damned door's at it again, I see." We needed to jiggle the knob to properly shut it.

"Yeah," I said by the typewriter. "The wood swells in winter." Like my joints.

"Yes, indeed." You took off your coat and hung it on the rack. "And nothing seems to stop it."

Standing, I held my arms over myself, warding off the cold. "Our door did that all winter at..." My eyes raked over your face; dark bags hung under your moony eyes. "You look tired."

"I'm not sure I should take the laudanum to sleep," you said, rubbing your forehead. "The languor seems to last long after I wake."

I frowned. "Doesn't it keep away nightmares?"

Your hand ghosted over the left set of dormant gills. "Yes, but I'll need it for pain, eventually."

I asked, "Can't you ask the doctor or a drugstore chemist for more?"

"Dr. Phillips would need to come visit me. Look at me. It might be okay now, but not later."

"Why? If you can't sleep, how can he tell by looking at your face or doing some test?"

You shook your head and rubbed your temple. The topic of Phillips seemed like a sore one, so I dropped it.

"I liked your singing," I told you, afraid I'd bothered you.

A thin smile. "Why, thank you."

When you went to bed, I came in and talked with you a bit on the opposite side of the bed, closest to the door. I planned to leave once you drifted off, but I fell asleep, too, curled by your side.

You said nothing of it when I woke up and you'd already gotten up. I found you sitting on the stone hearth, watching the flames. I sat in the recliner as the wind howled against the cottage walls.

You told me a little about the founding of your town, how a sea captain from your home discovered the Deep Ones and brought the fish-women back, and the men married them.

I said to you, "Tell me something the readings never said. Are Deep Ones people with a magical curse or another species entirely?"

You folded your hands in your lap, your thoughtful face ribbed by fire-light. "Both. The true Deep Ones, Deep One women, married sailors. Like sirens, I suppose, except instead of drowning their suitors, they fell in love. A different kind of suffocation."

Times like these, I caught a glimpse of your worldview, dampened with cynicism. I couldn't blame you. I don't blame you.

"Where do Deep Ones go when they need to mature?"

"The ocean." You removed the flat cap you used to hide your slow balding, setting it on the armrest. Fallen hair spiraled on the inside of the hat, along with something else pink and sticky.

"I understand that. Where in the ocean?"

"In my town, about half a mile out, there's a reef. Devil's Reef. Some-times, they stay there, but many go to an ancient city deep below."

"What is it called, Atlantis?"

"Y'ha-nthlei," you told me.

"What do the Deep Ones do, go into their own cocoons? Bubbles?"

You grinned, teeth pearly. Sharper by the fire. "I can't tell if you're being facetious. They acclimate to the water, let it fill their lungs, and let their body heal from the long change."

Some caterpillars take five days, others take three weeks. With you, I figured I might have a few years. More. Please, more.

Questions buzzed in my head, questions I wanted to ask based on what I knew of eldritch things. What was Y'ha-nthlei, the city under the tides, like? Was your Deep One mother alive? What did she look like? Were her scales green, blue, gray, or all? "How long does the entire trans-formation take?"

"Sometimes months, sometimes years. The first part can go rather fast, but it's letting everything develop that takes the longest."

It wasn't fair. How you had to grieve, how you trembled from fever and clasped sadly at your lost hair, but kept a strong front.

"I'm sorry about your hair. I saw, I saw the jar." In the back of the pantry, in one of the darkest, cobwebbed corners, you preserved some of your hair. It's still there.

You sadly smiled, eyes lantern-bright from the flames. "You must think me vain."

I bit my lip and shook my head. "Our hair's a part of us, since the beginning." Papa said I was born with a wave of silver-white curls, and I barely uttered a whimper. Mama feared I was stillborn when she, alone in the world, clung to me. "Even when I was little, I had my hair, even when I had nothing else."

"Nothing?" you asked softly.

My eyes ached when I stared at the fireplace. "Being a god's wife, that's something. I was something, something in some kinda providence. Not anymore. All I have is my body."

Peering up at the ceiling, you said, "That's something, too. I'll never have a body that's mine."

I blinked and asked you, "If your body isn't yours, whose is it?"

You scowled, though not at me. "My body has never belonged to me. Even as a child, I leased it. I had these moments of dissociation, of *feeling* myself with Father's hands, pulling taut vellum. It was on borrowed time. Ever since...and when I was thirteen. I was only thirteen, and then I was twenty-five. But I was always aware, all those years. Painfully aware. Just not in my body."

As I shuffled to stand near you, I didn't understand what you meant. Dissociation, feeling outside your body. Feeling yourself with your...my fears overtook me.

When we both sat on the stones by the fire, I gently held your wrist and smiled. "This is your body. This is you, and I'm glad to be here with you. More than anything. More than anyone."

You dozed off, leaning against me.

You've been gone quite a while, Azzie. Still, I feel the warmth of your cheek on my shoulder.

Before I started writing this current documentation of our past, I strolled on the sand and listened to the obscene promises of the ocean. Riches. Knowledge. If only I stepped in.

Instead, I went to the cove. The tide was low, and I found a perfect quahog pearl set on one of the rocks near where I fell into the water. Could've washed up, but it could've been left there; this particular stone was rather high to have a pearl roll on it with the tide. Others I've found inside the nearby abandoned lighthouse.

This one, though, it's the color of my eyes, and the fifteenth one I've found in that exact spot over the years, since you left to complete your transformation.

Have you seen the thank you notes I've left in bottles? I only see them dip beneath the waves, lost to me.

15. Azzie

When the first tooth fell out in spring, I spent the next few days in the bleary delirium of opium-mushed languor.

I stretched out on the bed, and you stood at the doorway.

"Vin," I murmured, already sleeplessly sleep-drunk. My arms were blissful lead.

"Yeah, I'm here," you replied.

I laughed. Not sure why. "Can you please help me unbutton my shirt?"

If only I could properly describe that wide-eyed look you gave me! I suppressed a laugh for a fear that you might think I was making a jest at your expense.

With a nod, you came over to the bed and sat on the side, regarding me with a curious stare. You shifted, raised a hand and let it fall to the top button of my white shirt. The collar itched against my closed gills. With both hands working like poetry, you unclasped the first button, and then another, another. Cold air hit the top of my chest.

I shuddered in delicious anticipation, but as soon as I did, I recoiled. And you stopped. After all you went through, I had no intentions of propositioning you. If anything were to happen, and I passively accepted I wanted an "anything" to happen, I wanted you to come to me. Though secretly, I imagined it was delirium that saw a hint of curiosity in your eyes, those eyes that I'd let drown me.

"M'sorry," you said. I bit down the urge to tell you not to apologize to me.

"No," I said. You pressed your lips together. "Nothing you did was bad. Keep going."

You helped me with two more, and I turned away to clumsily finish your work as you went to the dresser to fetch a gown. That dresser with a vanity mirror I avoided. When I heard you shift, you gave a soft gasp. Another shiver came when I knew you were studying my naked back.

"What is it?" I whispered.

"Nothing, seeing things," you replied, coming over and, on the other side of the bed, so you didn't see my front, tossing the gown by my side. You propped up the pillows, the sheets faintly smelling of lavender.

I pulled the gown over my head. I was careless and turned too early, and you caught a glimpse of me. Your look was solemn, but you didn't flinch or widen your eyes.

I nestled against the pillows, and you said, "I have an absurd question." Your face began to ruddy.

"Is it about my breasts?" I asked dryly.

To your credit, you're the most honest person I know. "Yes. Do fish-people need them?"

"Not fish-people. Deep Ones. Yes, they have them, and they feed the little ones with them."

"Your mama, did she give birth to you regular-like?"

"Yes." The image of me popping out of an egg is both disturbing and humorous.

You've made a habit of nodding off in my bed. I thought anyone being in this bed might bother me. It was my space away from the world. The months after I came here, when I slept with anyone, I never let them in the bed.

It's been a year since the last time, since I realized simple flings here and there weren't as freeing as I thought they'd be.

Shortly after a certain incident, when I was fully of my own mind again, I was not always this cold. I wanted to feel, to have others caress my flesh and feel like it was me inside my own body.

But it doesn't bother me when you're here, after you set the lemon tea down by me. You don't mean to doze with me, and you apologize once you wake up, and your face goes scarlet as a winesap apple.

"Sorry," you whispered. In the dead of night with the lantern long dead, I could barely see your face. "You were having a nightmare."

Your lips were so close. If I reached over not even a few inches, my bottom lip could brush against yours. The thought warmed the pebbled skin under my collarbone.

Yes, if things are to ever be different between us, I want you to initiate it.

I don't remember much of what I said after.

One night, the world was dark except for candlelight. Rain drummed against the roof.

I've done nothing with my life. I didn't love; I don't love. Because if I'm at a distance, I can learn and prosper without fear of pain. We learn by doing, by seeing the results, as messy as they are.

The stars don't foretell anything. They mock us.

We slept, and when I awoke, it was no longer raining, and the sun was out. I slept again, and before long, it was the afternoon.

On my back, I asked you, "Would you judge me if I told you I've been promiscuous in the past?" It mustn't make any sense to anyone but me. All I wanted was to assert my body was mine. I was the one who chose my lovers, chose what happened to me. When I visited the two brothers in the house closest to me, it was me who told them to take off their dungarees. Don't I live? Yes. Badly, I know, but I live.

And if you and I were to be together? Me, with what I'll become? I can only recall the books in Father's study. The ones he told me never to open. The ones I sometimes stole and kept in bed as I fingered myself, those musty texts with lovingly detailed illustrations of erotic conjoinings between faceless, thin-limbed human women and tentacled cosmic entities with jellyfish heads and barbed penises. I suppose, in the end, they were more interesting than the old Victorian magazines he had with a penchant for spankings and incest.

"No," you said, on your back beside me. Our elbows brushed together. "Can't see a reason to. There are really bad things."

"Like what?" I asked.

"People hurting others 'cause they can. That, I can't stand." Like that, you closed the topic on whether I should be judged. Oh, Vin, this bastard world has never deserved you. I must've looked ill because you rolled over and asked, "Do you need a hot cloth? Or some ointment?" My dormant gills were inflamed again.

I said, "That peppermint salve works well." You went and retrieved some. I wanted to tell you I could apply it, that you didn't need to worry about it, but truth be told, I always enjoy having your fingers on me. In me.

"I think we should try something," you said, tapping your chin.

"Yeah?"

"Do you think you'll feel better in water?"

I shake my head, sitting up on the pillow. A pang in my neck, but otherwise I don't feel so terrible. "Barely in freshwater."

"What about saltwater?" you asked.

"It's worth a try, I think. I feel better today."

You sucked in your bottom lip and worried it with your teeth. "Yes, I'd like to go out. I never used to—on today."

"Today? What's today?" I asked you.

"This is my birthday," you said. Flatly, as if it were nothing,

"Oh, how old are you?" I shook my head. "Sorry, that was impolite."

"Thirty-seven."

I blinked. "I never would've guessed." You smiled at that. Perhaps you thought I was being polite. "No, really. You were born in ..." I cocked my head and did the math. "1896. In spring."

Amused, you said, "Yes." You stood up from the bed and let me get up on my own.

I released a sigh. "Being a spring baby sounds lovely."

"When were you born?"

"In autumn, October. Such a gloomy time. Why don't I take you out on the town? It's been so long since I've done something like that. And East Providence is much better than the backwater place I came from. We couldn't even go into some buildings because my papa said they were full of shoggoths."

Your eyes widened as we crossed into the living room. "Were they?"

I shrugged with my hands, pacing to the front door. "I don't know! I was a little wary to look. You're the only person I know here who wouldn't be confused by that."

"I'm sure there are others who know. These secrets get around."

"They do. Quite frankly, I'm shocked that my hamlet has gotten away with as much as it has. You told me there were books on it."

"Yes."

"And yet, there's been no interventions of any kind." I shook my head and got back on topic, reaching for my coat on the rack. "Is there anywhere you'd want to go? You can pick the place. That is, if you'd like."

Your eyes grew hazy in thought as you moseyed to my side. "There was that restaurant you told me about. I think I'd like to try it. I've never been inside a restaurant before. We always ate our meals at home."

"All right. That sounds wonderful."

Indeed, it was.

16. VIN

You parked on a stretch of asphalt behind Lourenço's. When I put on the light purple dress you bought me, I made sure to study myself in the mirror and run my hands through my hair, and I caught my reflection in the auto window.

Hm. Not bad. A little fuzzy, but happy for once.

"This is the most splendid restaurant here," you said when we entered, voice an easy sigh. I loved when you spoke like that. My confident, sweet Azzie.

"It's beautiful," I said, looking over the red-gold interior, the silky tablecloths with delicate leaf patterns, and I meant it.

But the menu was overwhelming. I didn't know what most of the dishes were.

You asked, thumb poised on the sharp bottom corner of a menu. "Do you want suggestions?"

"Yes, tell me everything."

You cleared your throat. "I personally enjoy the fried cuttlefish with lemon and chips, but the deviled lobster is to die for. I could eat that any time of day. You know, they bake the fish in garlic here. It's customary to add wine, too, but of course, not with the ban. Do you like cuttlefish?"

You were speaking faster than usual, and I noticed a faint blush along your cheeks.

I shrugged. "I don't know. Can't say I ever tried it."

"What about lobster?"

I shook my head. "No, not that neither. We were close to the ocean, and sometimes we had some shrimp in our rice or johnnycake porridge, but that was about it."

You tapped a finger on your lips. "Do you like sweets?"

"Yes, at home, I ate a lot of toffee when I was little."

"The pão-por-deus is delicious." You swirled a finger in circles. "It's a golden brioche with coconut and vanilla. Or there's the king's cake."

"You seem like you're feeling a lot better," I said, teasing. No fatigue, no fever. I was happy this was one of your good days; I wished all good days for you.

You lowered your hands to the table and blinked, resting the menu flat. "I suppose this was just what I needed." I couldn't remember when the air began to feel easier between the two of us, but I was content with you.

I pressed my palm to my chin. "I don't want anything too expensive."

You held up a hand. "Please, don't think about that."

Eventually, I decided on the cuttlefish. When it came, I smelled the lemon and garlic baked into it, and my mouth watered. You got the lobster with a sausage cooked and stuffed inside it and layered with white cheese and glistening peppers.

"How does it taste?" you asked me halfway through the meal. I realized as I ate that I wasn't worried whether I was too fast or slow.

"It's good. I like it very much," I said.

You beamed, unguarded, and my heart lifted. "I'm glad."

I was more famished than I thought because I ate it all. When we left, my belly was satisfyingly full. Full. A strange, recent feeling.

I asked if we could go to the ocean again, promising not to tumble in.

The drive to the beach burgeoned with an energy I couldn't place. Not a terrible one, but as the sun began to lower, a tingle vibrated in my fingertips. Anticipation, waiting, but I didn't know what for. The worst kind. Despite that, I didn't feel afraid.

As sand crunched beneath us, I said to you, "I hope this isn't all because of pity. I feel like when it's not disdain from others, it's pity."

Softly, you murmured, "No, not pity."

As the late evening stars hovered over us in the dark stretch of sky, we shuffled through the sand to the cove. The cold bit into my cheeks, so I pulled a sapphire-colored scarf over them. Where the ocean moved into that mouth of land, you set your feet into the water and released a long, contented sigh. You didn't care if we got the inside of your auto wet; we'd done it before.

"Yes, this feels good." You looked down, and something caught your eye. A shrewd light twinkled in your gaze. You reached down into the water and picked something up, extending your hand to me.

"Look here, Vin."

Something glinted between your thumb and forefinger: a quahog pearl, round and deeply plum.

I took it and inspected it. When I tried to give it back, you waved.

I curled my fingers around it and pressed it to my heart. "It's beautiful."

You looked at me with dry humor, something I'd come to expect and appreciate from you. "I'll refrain from saying anything silly." I couldn't help but feel we came a long way from the first day we met; with the suggestion of a blush, you'd gone from aloof to playfully coy in a few months.

Still. I matched your tone. "Or sentimental? Are those one and the same to you?"

Your mouth parted. Apparently, I struck a chord, a glimmer of truth. The pinkness spread to your throat.

"I'm glad you like it. Really," you said.

My heart was too full, and I needed release.

Your mouth.

The scents of salt and a mix of sharpness and lilies overwhelmed me, and desire tugged at me.

Because I was taller than you back then, I needed to lean down. I came close, my bottom lip grazing against yours through my scarf. I didn't know what I was doing, so I barely nuzzled my concealed lips to yours and froze.

I thought about going back on it, saying it was a mistake. Something to save myself and my heart, bleeding, always bleeding, if you rejected me.

Before I could step away and pretend I wasn't doing anything, your arms lightly caressed the velvet above my elbows.

You waited, and I reached up to pinch the scarf that covered my mouth. I nodded to you, and together, we tugged it down to unveil my lips to you. Though I expected a chill, a hot flush crept along my cheeks.

I flowed forward, and our mouths met.

Your fingers ghosted over my elbows. I tasted the lobster and peppers as you opened your mouth to deepen the kiss, and my face prickled with heat. Thank goodness it was dark because my face must've been the color of a strawberry.

When your lips glanced off mine, your forehead brushed against my cheek, and your nose nudged mine as you craned up your chin. I realized you were rising with your toes. You swallowed thickly, and I had a lump in my throat.

After our kiss broke, you were flushed, and your eyes were bright. With tears, affection or sickness. Or maybe all three at war in you.

"We never did make those strawberry pies," I said, eyelids fluttering.

"Hmm. The market should be open." The walls between us, the dancing around what we meant, all of that was eroding. We swerved in these different thoughts together, in a dreamy haze.

After we bought cooking supplies, you drove us home, and despite it being night with our stomachs full, I showed you how to bake a pie until we were both covered in flour.

As we stood by the stove, I pointed to your face. "You have some on your nose."

You raised a hand to cup your cheek, but stopped short and laughed. "Oh, I must look even more like a ghost."

"You, too?" That was what the people at Dunwich would say. And often, as hateful as they were, I wondered if they were right. If I only half-existed alongside them, if that.

Your eyes widened. "I don't think you look like a ghost. Whoever told you that was wrong. And horrible. You're one of the most alive people I know." We used a towel to clean ourselves hastily, and though we couldn't stomach much pie we lounged by the hearth and ate a little.

"These are excellent," you said. "I haven't had anything so sweet since I was a child."

"What were you like as a child?" I asked you.

Silhouetted by flames, you laughed. "I sneaked out with Dad's pipes and cigars and went to the docks. By the time I was ten, I wore pants and smoked cigars."

"Sounds like you were wild."

"I was a rebellious brat." Your smile didn't meet your eyes.

"Did boys love you?"

You scrunched your nose. "No, not past when I was five. I was too bossy." You looked as if you wanted to add something to that, but you didn't.

I looked at my hands and swallowed thickly. "My childhood feels so long, like it took up most of my life. I feel useless sometimes. When I first...I thought about leaving, going to the forest. Letting what happens happen. Or sticking my head in the oven."

"Do you still think about that?" you asked me.

"No." Nowadays, if I ever feel that cold apathy, which tastes like old silverware... "I go to the typewriter or the sketchpad."

You brushed the hair out of my face, fingers lingering over my jaw. "Good." Breath whistling out of your nose, you said, "I feel disgusting."

Frowning, dusting flour off your nose and only adding more, I said, "I don't think you're disgusting."

"If I'm not horrible to look at now, I will be."

I said to you, "I doubt it."

"Why?" You sounded like you couldn't believe I didn't see yourself as you did: unlovable. Instinctively, you went to self-deprecation. "Please don't tell me I already look like a fish."

The universe was infinite. So, too, was its beauty, beauty that didn't adhere to the slim definitions made by men. Nothing could make you ugly to me. "I've seen monsters. I've loved them, but you aren't that. You're different. The people who live outside of human society, they might not walk the same or have the same gods, but they're people, too. Humans and Deep Ones are only two out of billions and billions of endless species."

Your eyes grew dark with contemplation. "Your sons."

I frowned. "I didn't mean my sons." To you, my sons were stains on the past I should've forgotten because remembering them hurt me. Like your past hurt you. Best not to bring it up. I might start to cry, and we might have an argument. I meant my papa and the people in town who resented me, who let him hurt me. "But I've been with someone different before."

"Don't," you whispered. A tremoring echo of when we first met. "Please, please don't think of me like him. It."

I fervently shake my head. "You're not."

You stared out then, closed your eyes, and took a deep breath. "Do you know what I fear, Vin?"

I leaned closer. "What is it?"

"I'll never have a body that's mine. My body has never belonged to me. Even as a child, I leased it. I was always on borrowed time."

Leased it.

I wished at the time that I knew what you meant. The horrible truth. "If you say it's yours, then it must be."

You hummed in thought. Once we cleaned up and properly washed our hands and faces, our clothes were still dusted in flour. By the sink, you leaned in close to set your cheek on my shoulder.

With a breezy sigh, you entered your bedroom and lit lanterns, candles, and incense. Inhaling the sweet fragrances of citruses and pomegranates, I lingered outside the door, unsure what to say and do. Waiting for an invitation.

"Vin?" you called, sitting on the edge of the bed. There it was.

"Yeah?"

"I like when you stay in bed with me."

My heart fluttered. So much was out of our control, but not this space.

Soon, we'd discover not even that was safe from what would come, but for now, it was a place of peace.

Yet, always, the air had a tightness to it, tug and pull. You'd taken off her shoes and stockings, and I saw the hint of something thin, easily torn, a glossy membrane between your smallest toe and its neighbor.

When I sat by you, your gloved fingers brushed against the front of my dress, tugged at my scarf, and you leaned in to lightly kiss me again. I reciprocated, my hand on the inside of your leg.

You pulled away, grimacing. "Hold on, my gums ache."

"All right," I said. And waited.

You were embarrassed to open your mouth because you didn't want me to see the gaps where some of your teeth once were. Your human teeth, anyway.

After you gave a nod, I peppered kisses along your chin and throat. You smelled of tobacco and salt and strawberries, but I also caught the sweat on your brow and the faintest hint of the pomegranate potpourri you must've set out this morning.

As I leaned away, I searched your face. Your mouth lifted in a smile, dimpling one of her cheeks, but I caught something forlorn. Your doubts. How we were on limited time, how relationships between girls like us weren't meant to last.

We were supposed to be dead and forgotten by now.

I didn't care about what the cosmos wanted for us, and I waited as you lifted your chin and appraised me, set a palm on the bed of curls on the side of my head and stroked your thumb against one strand. You took a deep breath, as if bracing yourself.

"Come," you said, raising your hands and wriggling your gloved fingers. "I'm tired of being dressed today." You began to tug on your forefinger, the fabric, with your teeth.

Before you could finish, I held up my hand, and you stopped. Stared at me. Waited. I curled both hands around your wrist, and you neither stiffened nor flinched, only watched me with those startling agate eyes. I licked my lips, nervous, and craned my head, so my wet lips almost touched the white silk of your glove you'd yet to remove.

In one fluid motion, I leaned closer, but instead of kissing your fingertips or knuckles, my teeth grazed the silk. The fabric yielded, but when my teeth glided along it, my imagination found it rough, yet another layer you shucked on to keep yourself hidden from the world. From me.

Slowly, finger by finger, I removed your false hand with my teeth, tugging until it yanked off, and I caught it.

"Goodness," you whispered. Unusually delicate. And I did the same for your other glove, taking my time, until they were discarded on the sheets. Between us.

"We don't need to do anything," I assured you, fearing I'd embarrass myself. That I already did. That I wouldn't know what to do with you if I tried. "Especially if you're tired. Or any reason."

"I want you," you rasped. "I don't know for how long I've wanted you, but I do."

To lighten the mood, this humid tension despite the air being dry and cool, I said, "We haven't known each other for that long."

It's melancholic now. In the very end, we'd only known each other for six months, and less then. One would think—I always thought if I were to love anyone, it'd take years for me to trust them enough with a kiss. I never felt much of an urge to even kiss a boy when I was a girl and started growing.

Your expression fell into something more somber as you sat up straighter.

Your eyes were half-lidded, and you opened your mouth as if to reply, but closed it and released a hum. "It really isn't fair, our height difference." You joked, "I'm not used to being with a woman who's taller than me."

As tall as I was, you were by no means short, though I always fondly liked to think of you as small. I was so used to being the tiniest person in a room or in the fields. Our bodies might have much of the same sinew for now, but we're so different, asymmetrical.

"I like it," I say.

"It is appealing, but I find myself at a disadvantage."

As we rested in bed on our sides, you balanced yourself on your elbow and looked down at me, those sharp corners of your eyes softening as you set a hand on my cheek. It was as if you were deliberating on what to do next. Cupping my hands in front of me, as if in prayer, I waited. Back in the living room, I heard the faint tick of your grandmother's clock.

Reaching for you, my thumb teased along your cheekbone, as if I were trying to smooth the blue shadows under your eyes. Oh, if I could, but you were beautiful to me. Always.

I took solace in the rise and fall of your chest, and as your breaths picked up, so did mine. I slipped my hand away, and your hand lifted and gently folded my fingers in your tender grip.

An envelope, sealed with the lightest of kisses.

That was when, for the first time in a while, that prickle came from between my thighs, a pleasant ache. That urge motioned on by the friction of your soft pink lips on my callused forefinger.

I don't know what possessed me—it might not be the best image, but I'd read some parts of *Hamlet* on your bookshelves, and I remember when Ophelia danced with a wreath of rue in her hair. To dance fiery and without abandon after you've lost everything. That was the energy that filled my chest when I craned my head and kissed you again.

As much as I craved tenderness, I was uncoiling and eager to explore and love and be loved with my body, in ways I'd never felt affection before from a single soul.

I leaned in close, so close both our lips grazed against one another, and I waited for your consent, mindful of your mouth pain. With a shuddering breath, I leaned back to regard your response.

You gave a small nod, and our mouths collided with each other. I was careful not to press too hard, but my right hand clumsily circled the first pearly button under your throat. I was surprised when you opened your mouth, and I let your tongue slide between my teeth and touch mine.

Electricity shot through me, the ache between my legs only growing. Mind too hazy and impatient to unclasp your entire front, I managed two buttons and slid a hand across the fevered milk of your skin, which was pricked with goosebumps under my palm. With a swiftness belied by your recent sickness, you raised a knee and positioned yourself above me.

At that angle, as our kiss broke, I could better see as I undid another button and slid and further traced my fingers along your skin until I found your breasts, and I teased my palm over your hardening nipple. When you tensed, I froze, but you released something between a gasp and a laugh.

Your eyelashes fluttered. "Please, go on," you said against my hair, lowering your lips to kiss the shell of my ear. The pleasure I felt below my navel, in that neglected part, became a sting, almost too much too bear.

I did, rolling your nipple under my thumb, and as sweat formed on my forehead and under my arms and breasts, you raised yourself up, so you were fully straightened and straddling my hips. As I released you, you offered a sly smile.

Your skin was wan. I didn't like seeing you so pale; I noticed the blue veins around your eyes and on your wrists. And you were thin, thinner than I'd ever been, even after being in nature. Your ribs faintly scalloped your sides.

I drank in that glimmer of your intense stare, that recipe of humor and contentment and hope.

Adjusting with my arms, I raised up, but not so much that I was fully against you. You rose a little, too, and, curious, I leaned forward to kiss your throat and collarbone, my hands brushing your hips, feeling the narrow jut of bone there. I had the silly thought that your nipples were the color of strawberries before they've fully ripened.

And then I lowered my lips, the salt of you on them, on my tongue, and I took your nipple into my mouth. With another short laugh, you furled your hands in my hair while I tasted you, my left hand gliding up your spine. I almost thought I felt it ripple.

I delighted most in the small sounds you made as I pressed my tongue against you. I took your other nipple between two fingers and toyed with it.

Though I was too aware that, with how much you raised yourself up, you were trembling a little. Exerting yourself, so we could manage.

"Vin," you gasped, and you swallowed thickly. Your eyes had a glassy sheen, like you might cry. "This is..."

Bashfully, I blinked. "Is this too much? Do we need to stop?" I was so worked up, my breaths were short and heavy.

Lines formed around your mouth, and you raised an inquisitive brow. "Do you want to stop?"

I deliberated on it, my attention falling to where dark hair collected at your thighs, curious to feel and taste you, to have you tense and moan and laugh with pleasure.

Once I leaned back, our gazes locked together.

"Like what you see?" you teased, a hand running across my shoulder and hovering over my collarbone, which was covered by the lilac-colored lace of my floral dress with silver lilies twisting along every curve.

I inhaled deeply through my nose. "Yes." A tad insecurely, I asked, "What about me?"

You gave me one of your rare tender smiles.

Even writing about it makes me stop for a moment; it's an expression I miss the most from you. If I did without kisses or sex for an eternity, I'd be sated with your smile.

"Yes," you said, "but I haven't seen much of you. Unless..." You sobered. "Unless you're uncomfortable with that."

I thought about it. I'd never let anyone see me naked on purpose, not in this context. I placed my hand near yours, some of our fingers overlapping inches from my heart.

When we kissed again, I pulled away again and saw your lips were getting redder and fuller each time we did it, almost the color of poppies.

Fearfully, I asked, "Am I hurting you?"

You grinned. "Oh, no. Please don't worry about that. They've always been sensitive." I admired your mouth; mine might've been pretty, too, but my bottom lip was healing from when I'd worried it last. Though I could've told you that I worried it even more since you got sick, as it was also its own distraction, I didn't want you to feel guilty for something beyond your control. "And besides, sometimes I like it to hurt a little."

"Oh." I felt out of my depths. New to this, I wasn't sure what you liked, and hell, I wasn't sure what *I* liked. The last thing I wanted was for this to be a disastrous fumble for you.

"Vin," you said seriously, "we don't need to do this." I appreciated your tentative approach, your consideration, but that need struck me, that urgency to act.

It was my turn to laugh. "I know."

Leaning back, I took your hand in mine and glided it to the buttons of my dress. I considered undressing myself, but I decided to give the control to you.

Slowly, with both hands, you unclasped the first button, the air hitting my lower throat, Another, and another, until you reached past my collarbone. Again, you met my eyes, and I'm not sure how to describe the motion I made—a slight curve of one side of my mouth, a ghost of a nod, and you continued until you reached the space between my breasts; I wasn't wearing anything there.

As if setting your hand on an unknown plot of earth, like when you go out to garden, at the start, you lightly put your fingertips on that plane of skin, in a loose semi-circle. Patiently, I waited and imagined that with your touch, you could feel my heart against your hand, against your veins, and its rhythm would flow back to your own heart. We could grow something together. The tensions in my shoulders loosened, and a wildness took root in me.

Often, I feared the unknown. Instinct, necessary to survive. But there were few things unknown to me except, as sad as it was, intimacy without conditions. Or love where, once riding the crests, I needed to wait for the troughs to plunge me into despair.

We'll get there, but even in our worst moments, you never used me, never manipulated me for your own ends. A low standard, perhaps, but we were both accustomed to torment. Any mistakes you made were because you were trying to help; it's hard when two people have traumas and, no matter how close the traumas, they have wildly different approaches to healing.

While you gingerly went to my shoulder and began to pull on one side, I tugged on the other, so together, we both managed to pull the dress down. It relented. Once the dress was rumpled on my stomach, and the cold air hit my breasts, I felt my nipples stiffen. Every sensation came alive, such as the feeling of the hair of your legs rubbing against mine.

You took in me, and, vulnerable, I took in you. I couldn't fully read the emotions flittering across your darkened stare. On my breasts were my silvery stretch marks, but also, the raised half-moons of scars.

"What happened?" you asked and squeezed my shoulder, your eyes flickering up to meet mine.

I offered a smile, realizing I wasn't self-conscious. "Teething little gods are more of a handful than regular babes. I know the scars are hideous." I didn't cow because I wasn't ashamed of these scars, I realized, because I loved my sons. Away from them, these were the last evidence of our love that I had. The stretch marks would achingly fade over several years, though the skin where they were was a little pinched and raised.

You shook your head. "No, no, they aren't ugly. Nothing about you is ugly." There was something taut and tremulous in your voice, like the A string on a viola.

I couldn't stand any of your anger about what happened to me, especially if it was directed at my sons. I didn't want to cause you more fury and grief. To you, anything that caused pain was refuse, an insult to be discarded. To have any affection for the past was weak because to reflect on that was to stew in the trauma. Bystanders of the unforgivable acts were equal to the abusers.

And yet, in the end, I know how you loved and missed your mama.

"Do you want to turn the lights off? Blow everything out?" I asked.

You blinked rapidly in surprise; I did quite enjoy catching you off-guard. "No. Do you want it off?" A spark of anxiety. I never asked about your fear of the dark; like everything else, I wanted you to reveal it in time.

"No." The light was the only thing I wanted on, so I could see you.

Wasn't there a surreality in this bitterly cold night where the two of us found joy and solace in one another? I never thought once about the awful past, nor was I submerged in self-doubt or grief; my world was your lips and hands. That dark time I ran from home with a shawl over my shoulders, I never would've imagined finding someone I could confide in, could reveal myself to in many ways—my eccentricities, my love of strawberries and words.

There we were, when you glanced your thumb over one of my breasts, and I arched into you. The closeness wasn't enough; I wanted to be closer, to be one with you, inside you, drink in your kiss.

You leaned forward. I thought you meant to kiss me, but instead you rested your temple against mine and released a sigh. I held you. I wondered if that was all, and I would've stopped, even if it meant neglecting the incessant pang of pleasure.

You looked up at me through your eyelids, and you reached down. I shifted on my side, and though you needed to sit up and stretch, you found that wet part of me, and deftly, you set a thumb near my clit and did lazy circles around it. I clung to you, then.

"Go on," you whispered in my ear. "Get on top of me."

"I like it like this," I replied, and you hummed in response. I released a gasp when you stopped your ministrations, setting your palm on my hip, and then ghosted it down to under my buttocks. With your gentle guidance, after we were both fully naked, you withdrew one of your legs and nudged mine above your own.

You scooted down, so we could align better. I shivered as you pressed yourself against me.

At first, all I felt was the soft skin of your pubic bone, mingled with hair, but then you adjusted, and we rubbed against one another. It was sweetly slow, and your eyes were downward, misted over in arousal or thought or some heady mix.

I cupped your breast with one hand, but I used the other to caress the sweat-slick curls away from your face, and you shifted to kiss my palm, and then buried your head against my collarbone, embracing me as you pressed into me faster. I reached around your shoulders, and soon enough, my pleasure began to peak. The sounds you made were raw, exquisite, and you soon tensed and shuddered, but you didn't stop, pressing kisses to my chest.

Soon, I climaxed, and it was a pleasure that came in waves, spreading from the center outward. I, too, shuddered and gave a sudden jerk, fatigue coming over me. With ease, you moved upwards and offered a kiss that felt chaste, given the circumstances.

Safe and content, I kissed your back, wanting to bask in the salt, flour, tobacco, strawberries, and pomegranates, but also that musk that was distinctly you.

My Azzie.

17. Azzie

That night with you on your birthday reinvigorated me. I wasn't healed, but I was hopeful.

For so long, I chased what could be progress in this rut I was in, unable to properly determine whether I lurched forward or backwards since I woke up in that lonely cellar three years ago. The rotting prison my father left me in.

That content ache in my muscles after our first night together went a long way in letting my spirits rise.

You rolled the purple pearl between your fingers and tested its weight in your palm. You asked me if I'd been with anyone. Scooting up, I kissed your forehead.

"Yes," I whispered. "It's...sometimes for a long time, sometimes for only a night."

Your eyes glittered in humor. "Oh, I knew that. You mentioned it. That's not what I meant."

"You mean, married?"

You paused. "Together, I suppose. In any way. Close. Living together."

I swallowed the sour taste in my mouth. I wasn't sure what to tell you. Saying either yes or no would've been true.

"Dr. Phillips pined after me for a few months, but I turned him down.

I never wanted anything complicated." As horribly self-conscious as I was about my body, I wanted to reclaim it, assert that it was my own. If I wanted to fuck someone, I could, however and whenever I wanted. But what happened after was exhaustion and frustration.

"Is that what we are?" you asked lightly.

"I'd say 'complicated' is a vast understatement."

"Yes," you replied. "I agree."

I hummed. "I was thinking."

"Yeah?"

"The circus came by train a few nights. They should have the tents ready."

"Right," you replied, "I think I saw something about that in the paper."

"Why don't we go tomorrow? With the depression, it's certainly no Barnum fare, but it's something."

You stared up dreamily at the ceiling. "I'd like that. Gosh, I can't even imagine what it's like. Have you ever been?"

"A few times." I can't say I've ever been too impressed. I've never been one to be easily thrilled by facepaint and stunts. But maybe you'd like it, and you deserve only good things. "There are trapeze artists, contortionists, fire-breathers, glass-eaters. And, hm, let me think, oh, lions and elephants." Lights and applause and women performers with sequined dresses and acrobatic suits.

As you napped, you kept the pearl secure in your grasp. What followed our dozing was a lazy morning. Birds warbled outside, and I quietly left the bed to brew coffee. When you came out barefoot, pulling your dress over your shoulders, I admired the curve of your ankle like I'd never done with another lover.

We spent the rest of the day in lazy contentment, sitting by the fire with our coffee mugs. Admittedly, such an easy morning and afternoon made me reluctant to go out when we could have our fun here; I thought about being back in bed with you that entire time, but I saw the light in your eyes when I curled your hair behind your ear and stood to ready myself in something other than a robe.

I chose a simple wool beret to wear, one with a false rose, a white blouse, and a black skirt.

And in blue, you were a slice of the ocean; more precious than any jewel. A hearty breeze greeted us when we sauntered to the auto.

At night, the circus teemed with yellow. The lights, the tents, some of the dresses and seersucker suits of fellow guests. In the distance erupted the trumpeting of elephants. You gasped.

I took my time walking to let you see anything, and I let you lead me to where you wanted to go. Didn't want to overwhelm you like in the city proper.

You are growing more confident with each passing day. I can see you blossoming independent of me. An artist, a writer. You weren't the same fearful woman who I found in the woods, and yet you were, you are. You are the woman you had to hide, the one you sheltered inside yourself, waiting for the right time to bloom.

You are beautiful like a star shower.

The tent where the shows happened had rows of seats like in the theater, and we sat in the back as clowns rolled on the stage with their unicycles and men swallowed swords and spewed fire. You smiled and clapped, and we locked eyes. My knuckles brushed against yours as I moved my hand to take a peanut out of the striped box you held.

"How do you like it?" I asked you when we were outside in the cool air.

You tossed a sweet grin. "It's quite a lot of fun."

"I imagine it's nothing revelatory."

"It is hard to be surprised when I feel like I've seen it all," you admitted. "But that's not true. Half my life's over, and there's much I haven't seen."

"Half? Are you sure?" I hope that one day you aren't so resigned to how temporary you are. It's true that we are all motes of dust in this cold universe, but that doesn't mean we need to act like it. As much as I've tried to fade, so the universe wouldn't see me and dig its teeth into me. I did my best to ruin Father's plans and become an inconvenience to the standard routine of things. If only I could've done more before I grew too comfortable.

Vin, how can I explain that when you came here, you both made me more comfortable and tore everything I knew apart. My routine, how I thought my body molded to the spaces I treaded across every day. That all has changed with you. I now see everything less unkindly. I see them when I never did at all. When they passed me by like water through my fingers. And I, too, was water passing away from the world, as if it were a cliff.

You offered a conciliatory smile. "With what my body's been through, I'd be surprised if I lasted into my seventies."

If only, in those glaring lights, I could've reached like I wanted to and wrapped my arm around yours. As a suitor might. The laughter around us cajoled me. Maybe I could do it, and everyone would assume we were childhood friends.

We came across an exhibit dubbed the "freak show." A list in elegant script, resembling like a menu:

Dwarves
Siamese twins
Wild men
A bearded lady &
An African tribesman with a hideous mouthpiece

My chest tightened. Unpleasantly so. I didn't like seeing bodies as spectacle. People made into objects, as my body was once an object separate from my soul. Before, this was something I never thought about in cinema and entertainment until I watched *Freaks* and felt that tug of empathy toward people talking about marriage, birth, and their loves.

My mother and hundreds in my hometown could fit in a show for spectators to gawk and laugh at. Your sons, too. And I saw how some of the passerbys glanced at you and whispered to themselves.

Look at that albino. Freaks.

Yes, I can't help but feel singular, even when I know my people in the sea are numbered in the hundreds of thousands. Am I their kin, or am I yours? Your lover? Your woman? Deep Ones don't truly have genders, initially. They change sex as needed, and only when they started marrying human men were they called brides.

You continued to munch on peanuts from a small box. When you looked up and met the eyes of someone gawking, you wiped your mouth with the back of your hand, self-conscious. Simmering, I glared at everyone around us.

I know you touched the so-called divine and it was cruel and traumatizing.

If I could be a god of the stars or sea, I'd be an avenging one.

For you.

I wanted that power, and for a fleeting moment, I thought my meta-morphosis might not be too terrible; being a Deep One would make me more formidable, more powerful, than I was.

"Go on," you murmured. "I've seen you looking at my arm."

At your request, I looped my arm around yours as we walked to the auto.

We drove home in the dark in an easy silence. Chin on your palm, your breaths plumed against the window.

I pulled over on an unobtrusive patch of grass close to the road. I was ravenous for the touch of your gentle skin on mine, that mild taste as I kissed your throat and your pulse fluttered under it.

Languidly, you threaded your hands through the ripples of my hair as you freed it with the tug of some pins. I didn't care where they fell; damn them. Your kiss was less hesitant than before, and your teeth plucked at my bottom lip and retreated, only for me to cup your chin in my hands and have our lips meet once more.

We didn't even make it home before we were crossing our arms to reach under each other's dresses. I slipped my hand in your bloomers, not patient enough to fuss with undressing and you did the same and brushed my clit. I released a soft gasp. When I cupped you in my hand, you were pulsing wet. The thrill of being in the auto on a less traveled road only intensified my need.

We leaned into each other and mutually brought each other to climax. With your collar disturbed, the first button popped open, I kissed the top of your collarbone.

I was far from tired, and when we went home and got out of the auto in the complete darkness, you slipped your hand in mine and leaned your chin on my shoulder, your breath on my throat, as I slid the key into the lock.

We fell on the sheets, you on top of me, and I phantomed my hand under your dress to clasp your breast. Our lips kept meeting as we clung together, as if it were the last night we'd ever have.

We wore each other out, naked and facing one another. You took my hand and kissed one of my knuckles. My back ached, like I slept on it wrong. I ran my fingers through your curls, content in the warmth between us.

Once you drifted off, I left the bed and ate some of the pie in the oven. Too soon, though, my stomach roiled with a sharp pang, and I darted to the washroom.

Immediately, I threw up in the commode. Half-standing and trying to make it to the sink, I didn't even have time to flush and wipe my mouth with a wet cloth before I heard a rip and squelch.

The top of my back split apart, and a new spine ruptured out of it.

18. Vin

We were wrong to think we won, that we conquered our ghosts. The gods never let us have it so easy. Or is it us who, in our need to lead simple and happy lives, underestimate the tragedies of the universe?

Like Orpheus, we must go forward, no matter what small part of us wants to look behind us.

But we looked.

If the gods are stardust and mystery, you became like a god to me. Not in the sense that you were untouchable or perfect, but when I saw your reflection in the small parts of my life, I loved them. I knew myself better and was content. Our intimate rituals became prayer and communion.

Now, I could only feel guilt for ever feeling jealous of you and your beauty.

Taking care of you was an adventure and new routine in one, a welcome distraction. That, your driving lessons, the gardening, and the writing—it was all making me feel more rounded and whole.

When I awoke from a scream in my dreams, goosebumps on my skin, sheets at my waist, the sky outside was gray. I didn't hear you, so I stood, taking your blue robe off the door and gliding it over my shoulders.

When I found you, you rested on the washroom tiles in the dark.

Though panic hammered in my throat, still sleep-drunk, I didn't understand.

A flash of hip, part of your leg, stones jutting out of the water the shadows made of the space.

You were naked. Your shuddering breaths were heavy. Stones in water.

And then, I saw blood glistening on the tiles, along with something pink and viscous.

When I called to you in the ghoulish shadows, your breath caught.

"Vin, please." Your words are muffled, a croak; you hadn't grown all your new teeth yet, but it hurt you to speak too long without opium.

Turning the light on, I came to lightly touch your shoulder, and I saw it.

Your spine was moving and glowing, like a bulb full of fireflies. Your body was full of lightning, like a tragic maiden in a morality play. Bubbles flowing in water, that's what the bioluminescent, toxic-blue flecks were doing. I was viewing an entirely different world on a bridge of bone, now that your skin, only here, had become translucent.

And inside you, I also saw black tendrils writhe, as thin as blades of grass, and prick your skin from the inside.

That was at the small of your back. The top—it looked like you'd been cleaved in two from behind.

Already, above, you had a fin about as long as my forefinger. At least, that was what had already emerged. Your fin was divided by those black lines and slick with blood where it burst the skin; slowly, it grew between the cliffs of your shoulder blades. Already, the flesh of your back, crawling like alien grass, was merging with it, mending the sloshing gash of a wound the erupted fin created.

You breathed in long, forced breaths. You squeezed your eyes closed, and I couldn't imagine the amount of strength you exhausted to keep from weeping in agony. The transformation wouldn't kill you, but it was doing its damnedest to break you.

And yet, Papa would say it was merely a natural progression, and nature has no care for what we want.

Bodies don't care. Gods don't care.

Eyelids snapping open, you looked at me with red-rimmed eyes. Azzie, you, in the most atrocious pain of your life, needed me to help you, and I didn't know what to do.

"W..." You grit your teeth and tried to stand, would've slipped on your own blood if I didn't reach out and clutch you close to me. Your blood and sweat soaked into the robe.

I looked at the tub. Not saltwater, but with an idea, I helped you sit on the commode, shot forward, and twisted the knobs for the water. I heard the squeaking of your shivers against the porcelain.

In this brackish world, humans adapt. We accept the worst as normal. I accepted Papa's treatment of me in the lonely house as ordinary. His condescension, his neglect. I wasn't sure what was more horrible, but I counted my blessings. I told myself it could be worse. He could hit me.

So, too, would you come to accept this with the same dry humor with which you accept everything. You'll grow used to blood, and so will I.

That was what I told myself, and it was somewhat true. Pain and trauma can become normal, until one can't tell what's a natural response and what is an act of over-vigilance.

"Come." I reached out and shakingly helped you into the tub.

You sloughed down, the water immediately turning a dark red-brown.

Your breaths were heavy and short, and your eyes searched mine.

"What is it?" I murmured.

"Vin," you said groggily, rubbing the side of your face with a wince, "you really, truly blew my back out."

See?

I tsked.

"Look, look at it. I can feel it." I couldn't tell what you meant until I looked at the fin and the wound. Your healing skin quickened, fusing itself to your new part. A seal.

"God," was all I could say. I noticed something like glass in your mouth. "Wait, Azzie, can you open your mouth?"

You did for me, and I saw them in the back: teeth. Thin as needles, but they reminded me of glass. All different sizes. Like those of some carnivorous fish.

When you closed your mouth, you groaned. "They're cutting into my gums."

And your tongue, too.

Standing, I went to the sink and opened the drawer, fishing out a silver thimble to secure on my thumb. When I leaned over you, you shook your head.

"That won't get rid of them." And indeed, if I were a lady with sharp teeth, I might not want to relinquish them. They could come in handy if danger arose.

"Okay," I replied, hand still hovering. "Show me the most painful part."

You shut your mouth, lowered your eyes to the bloodied water. Rose a hand, gently clasped my wrist. I let you. Let you guide me as you opened your mouth again.

You stopped just before the thimble grazed your bottom lip. A flash in your eyes. Worry. Worry of what I'd do? That I might cut myself?

Tentatively, you poked your cheek, and I guided my thumb inside your wet mouth. You leaned closer, head breath warm on my neck. Craned your head up so I could see better, water sloshing on the floor, on me. I didn't mind.

As I slipped inside you, I roved the thimble over one of the pearly, thin daggers, grinding against it. You released a low noise in your throat. As I thrusted my finger against the tooth, it gave way, softened. My neck seized from how long I held myself like that, but it felt good to have you close. To hope I was offering some measure of comfort as I swore I saw your fin flex and twitch as I worked.

"Better?" I asked when I finished, pulling away. Your cheek templed out where your tongue carefully roved the dulled teeth, and you nodded.

"Could you do that with a giant fin?" you joked, but your voice was thin.

A bashful grin. "I'm not sure. Maybe. Stranger things have happened."

I wanted to rub your back, but instead I squeezed your shoulder. You regarded me with sorrow.

"I'm sorry about the mess," you said dully.

My initial reaction was to gawk. Apologizing to me for bleeding on your own floor. I wonder if your father made me say sorry for something similar. "Don't worry about that. Doesn't bother me none." We lapsed into silence until I told you I'd fetch you a robe you could wear backwards. I'd have to modify your other clothes.

After I fed you laudanum and helped you dress, I thought you might want to be alone in bed. You often liked being alone when you were struggling.

"Stay with me." You burrowed your head above my knee, taking my hand in yours and ghosting your lips over my wrist.

I pressed my hand to your hair, which was the thinnest it'd ever been. "I will." My thumb glanced past another patch of your scalp that was smooth. "I thought you said water without salt wouldn't do much."

"It didn't, but it helped," you murmured. "I appreciate it." I now understood your frustration when I thanked you for basic kindness. "This isn't much compared to the ocean." Wistfully, you continued, "My mother's probably in the sea by now, you know. She's left like they all do."

"Are you going to leave?" I asked you. Dread clenched in my stomach at the idea.

You looked up at me. "Do you want me to?"

Yes, I should've said, after seeing the anguish you were in, but I was a selfish idiot fearful of abandonment. I couldn't help how my voice broke. "No. I couldn't stand it."

Your gaze was resolute. "Then, I won't."

"But what happens if you stay?"

You gave a small shrug and momentarily grimaced. "I imagine the process will be longer. It's like tadpoles."

I asked, "Tadpoles?"

You held up a hand. I waited as a clock ticked and rain pattered the front window. "They're supposed to be in the water to mature before they become amphibious. Mother..." You trailed off, the lines around your mouth darkening with memories.

"A tadpole," I said, trying to lighten the mood. "You don't have a cute tail."

"Yes." Your finger traced circles into the dirty water. "Hope my adorable personality can make up for it."

I wrapped my head around what you told me. "But if you need to be like a tadpole—if they aren't in water, they die."

Your jaw clenched. "I won't die."

"How do you know?"

With conviction, you said, "Because I didn't fight to live so I could die to a goddamned curse."

"Sleep, and..." Your old words echoed in my head. "Focus on your healing."

A pause. Your eyes drifted, and I'm not sure what brought the next question. "What did your sons look like?"

I hummed. "With Wilbur, his legs started to bend, and his feet—they were cloven, like a goat's. That's what I would best describe him as, like a goat, with thick silver hair on his legs. I know you said not to compare people to animals. I was fond of that. As a girl, the goats always followed me around."

You blinked slowly, perhaps imagining what he looked like. You looked down at your seafoam-colored robe. "Did he wear people clothes?"

"Oh, yes, and he was even taller than me. It was hard finding things to fit him, so I had to fix some of Papa's old clothes."

"That must be pretty tall," you said.

My throat bloated with memories. "And he was my shortest son. And my other son, I don't know how to describe him."

"Hm." You drifted, and I took your hand in mine. "It must've been difficult for all of you. Being outsiders."

"Yeah," I said, "but there were good things, too. Since most of the people thought I was a witch, they left me alone."

You laughed, and as you dozed, I settled by your side.

19. Azzie

I HAVE COMMITTED A TERRIBLE WRONG TO YOU, VIN, AND I understand if you'll never forgive me.

I'm only glad you're back. I might deserve this happiness, but you deserve to be safe.

For many long days, my body sent strange twinges down my arms and legs. At the dinner table, I went to reach around and touch my fin; even today, the fin almost breathes. It has its own pulsing veins, poor circulation.

I decided I needed to smoke, and so I retrieved some from the desk with the radio, which I started to think of as your radio, since you used it far more than me.

And what's more? My gills cracked open.

I sat at the dinner, bit my teeth down on the Nat Sherman cigar, lit a match. Once I sucked in the smoke, I accidentally swallowed some down my throat. You had come out of our bedroom, and you paused. I thought it was the sight of me smoking that surprised you, but then you pointed to the side of your neck, and I saw it in the corner of my eye.

Smoke curled out of my gills. It tickled.

Once I lifted my eyes to meet yours again, we shared a laugh.

I always love that way your laugh lines deepen when you're happy.

Seeing how you didn't care beyond concern, didn't see me as a repulsive monster, it was a little easier normalizing my changes.

Despite my condition, I felt strong enough to try to fetch the newspaper by the mailbox. Breathing was more strained because though the gills did the same as my mouth, inhaled oxygen and expelled carbon dioxide, it felt like I was leaking. Air, blood, everything.

"I can do it," you told me, frowning. "Don't strain yourself."

I insisted. A matter of pride, maybe. If I couldn't do something as simple as checking the mailbox, I might as well not try anything at all. I spent years confined, and I wouldn't let this cottage, the home I found with you, become a prison, a coffin to lock me inside as it descends into the ground.

I had to be quick, of course, especially coming back, since I wasn't sure how anyone else would react to my fin and gills. My guess was not good.

Going outside was hard when it was such a dry cold, though thankfully spring made some of the late mornings and afternoons bearable. A frog slapped its legs through a nearby puddle as I collected the news. As I picked the rolled paper up and unfurled it, the front page caught my eye.

A grisly death only obscured by the graininess of the photograph; a body surrounded by what looked like fallen books. And it'd, he'd been utterly mauled.

I'll spare more details, but I read the headline and some of the story:

Experts Try to Identify Goat-Like Abomination Torn Apart By Dogs in Miskatonic University Library

All signs have pointed toward the small town of Dunwich, best known for its scenic hills and chicken farms.

Wilbur Whateley, a deformed "man" who appeared in the town years ago after the clandestine pregnancy of a missing woman. The man identified as his grandfather had no comment. Whateley is best described as a creature, his devilishly contorted features more goatish than human.

• • •

My ashen heart slammed to my feet, and I almost vomited.

Even if I could never understand your fondness for your sons after what they must remind you of, I never asked for this. Vin, if only there was a limit to the grief the gods ask of us.

You can't know, I thought then, imagining I was sleeping by your side, ghosting my fingers over your arm. You can't know. This will break you. How foolish I was to think I could hide anything from you, especially the death of your precious son. If only I could not be so selfish, if I could accept that I will never be forgiven.

20. Vin

LATE THAT APRIL, I WAS REELING FROM BEING BACK HOME AT the cottage after a stint in the woods. It didn't feel real. Nothing did. What did I even do the day I left? What I saw in the forest after I ran away from you, I can't explain, despite remembering it all.

Retrospect helps, but I don't know what was illusory and what was real. I can say what was literally before my eyes, as in what I saw, but I cannot say what it meant or if it was truly there.

I should start a few days before. I've never been one for setting schedules, but helping you set a clock on your body:

7:00 a.m. - Make you breakfast and give you a glass of water, full of salt.

7:30 a.m. - Check gills, fin, & mouth for infection.

12:00 p.m. - Make you lunch. You're not used to a meal during lunch.

9:00 p.m. - Give you laudanum. Rub your shoulder until you sleep.

Your face was ashen, and you hated the feeling of clothes on your skin, but thankfully, you were able to eat a little fish most mornings. I asked you if this was cannibalism, and you said that many fish ate others of their kind.

Lunch, sometimes. Dinner was somehow harder, and you mostly slept through the evenings and nights. If you'd sleep at all. I wondered what it'd be like for you if you were in the sea, with how dark it must be down at the far bottom. My Azzie, with your nervous bird movements, always rising with the sun. You didn't seem like the kind of person who'd take to darkness. Always, you needed some light on.

"Yes, it's dark in many places down there, away from the cities," you said to me one night, rasp fighting against the heavy rain.

"Dark and lonely," I muttered.

"Dark," you replied, "but not lonely."

That fateful day: At the kitchen table, you nibbled on your food slowly. As birdsong came from the trees outside, I cleaned the dirty dishes and went to scrub the bloodied towels in the outside basin until my arms ached up to my elbows.

I've been thinking of how best to address what happened.

My son, Wilbur. Seeing his name written like this, I tried using the typewriter to spell out his name as I wrote about him. I couldn't.

"I took some things out to the burn pile," you told me that day in bed. I didn't think anything of it until I looked for the newspaper later. I liked having an eye out into the world.

How swift you could be when you needed to lie to me. To protect me. I didn't know what it felt like to be protected.

Earlier, hand on the table by the front door, I had frowned and called, "Where's the newspaper?"

When I went to the bedroom door, sitting up precariously on your side, you gave me a placid curl of your lips. "I tossed it out. Nothing of interest." Something dark boiled in your eyes. You thought a smile could fool me. Did you think me simple, after all?

After—after all we'd been through, I resented you.

"All right, then. How's your back feel?" I asked you, sitting on the bed.

You frowned. "It's itching terribly."

"I'll get the salve," I told you.

"Thank you," you said, and something was in your voice. Something low and sad. The hairs on the back of my neck stood on end.

The skin around the fin had taken on a grayish tone, and you told me that was normal. The fin, however, was a brilliant collage of olive-green and a brighter emerald, with a touch of blue.

After I gave you the salve, helped you apply it where you had trouble reaching, I stood up and walked out, looked back as aloe and peppermint filled the air. Your fin twitched, and you fidgeted with your hair, so thin I could see your scalp.

You were keeping an eye on me now. I'd need to be fast.

I waited for you to come to the kitchen, eat, and return to bed.

Eventually, you drifted off into sleep, but your naps were always light and troubled, so I didn't have much time. I crept along the house and found myself at the back door. With held breath, I eased myself out, careful to not let the screen door creak. I guided the screen door against the stone, worried the wind would knock it back, but I was all nerves.

A light drizzle sprinkled the grass. In the center of my vision was the fire pit you used for paper and wooden trash, so I treaded carefully until I found the newest paper, still fresh and hurriedly tossed on the ground. Bending, I picked it up. The day was cool, and birdsong floated from the trees. The paper was charred at the edges, but damp.

Ah. You tried to burn it, but the rain stopped you.

I stared at the front page, that despicable photo they took of my boy. That was all it took, but the headline flashed white in my sight when I blinked and let the world turn dark for a second.

Experts Try to Identify Goat-Like Abomination Torn Apart By Dogs in Miskatonic University Library

I read further, and I stopped at the photo.

Wilbur.

Willy.

My soul died.

I dropped the paper, and it scattered a few feet away as a horrid chill passed through. Shaking, knees weak, I collapsed, only reaching out to keep myself from fully feeling the impact. My teeth jerked back in my mouth.

I left him and never came back.

In my escape, I never realized he was a victim of Papa's plans, too. In letting Wilbur be my savior, I didn't save him. His life was over, and mine was, too.

I left him, and he died.

I left him to die.

It couldn't be true, shouldn't be true, but it was.

What kind of person was I to leave and not beg him to go with me? What sort of mother?

The wind violently twisted around me, and the screen door was thrown back, slamming against the cottage wall.

I gazed upward through blurred eyes. You stood at the back door, holding open the screen door.

Immediately, instead of comforting me, you jumped to your own defense. To your credit, you didn't try to deny what you'd done. "I was afraid—I didn't want you to be—"

I snapped, "Stop." You did. A heavy, long silence. Your pulse thrummed visibly in your neck, your gills shuttering. I struggled not to throw up my own heart. "You never cared about him. Why would you?"

Hand on the frame, your mouth worked. "It's not that I don't care. I just don't know how..." Your face was clammy with both sweat and rain.

I whispered, "I can't believe anything you're saying." I couldn't tell if you heard me as you stepped out to join me by the ashes, all burned except for the grisly black-and-white image of my son's violent death.

The boy I fed strawberry cake and wheeled around in a wagon.

Abomination.

That was what the paper called him. Twisted wretch.

My breasts ached, remembering teeth.

I shouldn't love him, you told me.

"What do you need from me?" you asked, deathly quiet.

I drew myself to my full height, facing away from you. "Nothing. I don't want you around me." That hurt you, which was why I said it.

Your voice rose a pitch. "Vin, please. Look at me. I'm sorry. Please don't look away. I just—"

My nails cut into my palms, and my arms itched with that need to hurt them to feel, to have a little control. "Need me to move on. Need me to pretend I'm not hurt by what happened. Why, so you can fuck me without feeling guilty? So you can pretend you're in bed with someone normal, and not, not whatever I am?" A freak who gave birth to monsters. A lonely godswife who escaped her due. The ugly idiot who lived in an old shack, who was only worthy of disgust and pity.

You tried to fight back, my eyes fuzzy, blurry with new tears and rain. "No. Normal? You know I don't care about that. Look at me."

"I was an idiot to trust you." No, I was an idiot becoming so lost in caring for you, loving you; those had become one, and in turn, I'd become more isolated. I trusted you to be my outside eyes, and you decided what I should and shouldn't know about my own children.

If you wanted me to look at you, I would.

Your face was slick with wax. Sweat, rain, not tears.

You flinched back.

I said, "You think I'm like you. That I can be emotionless, forget everyone I loved like they're trash. Will myself into amnesia."

Shoulders tense, withdrawing, your voice was dangerously low. "Is that how you think of me? You think I don't remember what it's like to be made little and scared, that I'm dead inside?"

When I did say I forgave you, much later, I'm not sure I meant it. Did I ever say that or did I dream of it? Devastated, I only wanted a tentative peace back; life was too chaotic and sad as it was.

I do forgive you now. You weren't trying to erase a part of me, take away my grief because it inconvenienced you; you only tried to help me cope the best you knew how, to erase, to try desperately to forget, but it was as if we were in that fabled splintered tower, and once it crumbled, well. We came from the same stone, but our languages were lost to one another.

"Maybe," I said. That hurting place in me got hard and cold. I hated how it felt; toxins pulsed from the core of me.

Your expression was stern, but tears shone in your eyes. Yes, that's right. I remember now, I was wrong; you did cry. "Then, go. I'm not going to argue with you." You thought I'd go back inside to weep, maybe sleep in the guest bedroom again.

I needed to leave. I couldn't look at you anymore, couldn't be here in this cottage, this world, which sloshed with blood and despair and loneliness.

You stepped closer, and I wrenched myself from the spot.

"Get away from me," I rasped.

Snapping my gaze away from you, I dashed around the cottage. In your condition, I didn't expect you to follow me.

"Wait, where are you going?" you asked after me, not expecting me to actually go.

I ignored you. I planned to never return. I planned to die or something much, much worse.

"Vin, Vin? Let's talk about this, please—" The wind gnashed away your words.

As I passed the front corner of the house and dashed past the front porch, you tripped and tumbled to the ground, hardened by cold. I could feel the tremor of your knees and chest hitting dirt.

You cried out in pain, and I felt the clatter of your bones.

Blinded with tears, I fled farther into the woods.

21. Azzie

THOSE THREE DAYS YOU WERE GONE, WHEN I RAN TO TRY TO find you—they almost killed me.

I can't say I didn't deserve it. It was three days after, yes, three soggy newspapers stacked by the mailbox.

The air grew warmer, but that meant when the rain came, it became a flood.

As it happens, rain, even with seawater in the clouds, is free of salt, but I nevertheless felt a little less tired. My fever subsided, and I could think without the dull pangs or mind-fog. The relief was minimal. As I thought about where you must be, and how cold and soaked you were, my throat threatened to burst. I shook.

I was an idiot. I'd failed you.

And you were right. I didn't understand you, didn't have the same courage as you. I found courage in moving on, in getting through the day. And you did that while connecting with the past.

If I let myself dwell on what was done to my soul and body, I'd snap in twain. Besides, it felt uselessly cruel to keep stepping back into the hateful past, those twelve years since I was a thin wisp on the docks of the Harbour.

As I was drenched, a madness entered me. With my gills open, water also poured past those feather-like, fleshy threads of blood and fell down my throat.

I was more alive, but also desperate. I felt like I was becoming feral. I ran and ran and ran. Though my condition made me tired, a burst of nerves came over me, and I took every advantage of it.

I needed to find you. To think you'd die out in the wilderness—starve from exposure, get struck by lightning, I couldn't stand it. You hadn't survived what your bastard father and no-good town did only to die like this.

I betrayed you, and I lost you. It was foolish to think you were ever someone who belonged to me. No one was an object, and besides, in the end, we were all alone on tiny rocks the gods manipulated or destroyed for their amusement.

At home, they were the world, these gods. Two in particular who lived in the sea as consorts. But I assumed, as I went to Miskatonic, that though the occult was a fetish for some, in the world at large, industrial and advanced, these were fringe fancies.

And anything, anything, that happened as a matter of these beliefs was merely a scientific phenomenon that hadn't yet been studied and given a proper name.

Desperate, so desperate to deny the inevitable. The sundering of humanity.

On this insignificant planet, we were never meant to love. To have it, hold it, keep it. Everything decays. Especially love. Foolish. Selfish. Emotional. Infinitesimal in the massive cosmos. In the end, it would never leave an impression. When the Earth was gone, all the poems and epics about love and heroism would die.

And then you flooded my mind, Vin, stronger than those stubborn torrents of despair.

If you died because of me after the horrors you endured, I'd never forgive myself, but it was more than that. No one deserves to live more than you, Vin. Not because you were hurt, but because of what I've seen you get out of the world, and what, even if it hasn't earned it, the world can gain from you being in it.

Yet, though you remained, it took some time to get up. My mind, there, in an endless mire. Grief-blue and hopeless. This was why I never got fanciful or dreamy. Wandering into abstraction only invited the gods in.

When I considered the state of the universe and our place in it, I ended up here: nowhere, as nothing.

Since I was born, I've lived on the periphery, my black boots at the threshold, nails digging into the door. Couldn't linger in my father's study or listen to what he and his eccentric friends spoke about; some knowledge wasn't meant for women, he said with contempt, because they were too physically and mentally frail to handle it.

He loathed me, raked his eyes down my gangly body with contempt. It didn't stop him from stealing my life from me, so twelve of my years weren't mine. Will never be.

The idiot, the bastard.

He deserved to die. I'm glad I killed him.

No matter my regrets, I won't feel shame for that, ever. If rage and revenge are ugly or monstrous, then so be it.

I was his puppet, and am I strong for defeating him? Would I be weak if I hadn't been able to? How many girls, the daughters of errant scientists and mad occultists, fell for that same logic and felt broken?

I wove through trees and bushes, no longer naked from winter. My clothes and skin snatched on briars. Thankfully, despite my skin peeling horribly, it seemed to be thicker than it once was.

My gums ached, and my voice was rough, but I called your name. Birdsong and rain answered, but not you. I loathed hearing the warbles from above; even after living here for three years, they were strange noises to me. I began to climb steep inclines, concealed by blankets of dead leaves and fallen branches.

One wrong step, I'd crash down. What might've taken me a few minutes stretched on. I needed to go from tree to tree, using branches as leverage. Weak from not eating, I trembled, my arms and legs unreliable.

Hours into the search, as the day began to dim, despair set in. I was faced with the choice of heading back or continuing on. My body, my stupid, worthless body. Burdensome, not fitting into the space right. No longer could I simply dart through the woods. I had to be careful where I turned, so my fin wouldn't bump into anything or get scratched.

I imagined if I hit the fin just right, it might rip off my spine; it ached and throbbed. Unpleasant, to say the least, but my burgeoning body was half-formed and both harder and softer at once. I've never quite been able to lift my feet off the boundary of two things. Be hard or soft. Wear trousers or lipstick. I've defied the idea that I've had to settle at all.

Everything was more sensitive against my skin, so the pain as branches jammed into my legs was magnified. The wetness of the area didn't bother me so much, except I was clumsy in this new body.

I slipped in the mud and rain, my body slamming into the earth, loose, curved teeth jiggling in my mouth. My left ankle ached, and I wasn't sure if it was twisted. When you experience such pain often, it can be hard to tell an injury from the usual.

"Please," I said to my body, "you goddamned useless pile of shit. *Help me.*"

A stinging pain in my mouth turned into an agony that radiated to my jaw. I was teething, and I spat out another tooth, followed by a bloody string with pus and mucus.

I wept.

The nearly six months we've known each other have felt longer because of the times I've held my tongue, afraid to push you into anything you were unprepared for. Had I rushed us too deeply into intimacy? Had your confessions to me eclipsed my ability to treat you like you deserved?

I was stupid. I misused my body once I got it back. I could be greedy and surly.

I wanted everything. Like Father said, a glutton. He'd always punish me. Lock me in the closet. Snap a ruler over my knuckles.

That bastard. No, he can't be right. A man like him would think there's a way to love too much. After years of being chastised for occupying space, I decided to live.

Where has that gotten me? I wondered. My body didn't belong to me, and it was rebelling. I'd gone against the path laid out for me, that cold, terrible, barren plan, but that led me in the mud, alone. Left me unable to do anything for you but try to obscure things you deserved to know, if it meant keeping trauma away.

That was what I did with myself, and it didn't work. I tried it with you, every distraction, nice food and new clothes and gentle sex, and it ruined you. I ruined you.

My ways of coping were to forget, not let any intrusive thought in. I had to patch over twelve years, pretend I'd gone from being a meddlesome thirteen-year-old to a grown woman who graduated from college with all this knowledge about Avicenna and the nuances of essence and existence. The only woman to graduate from Miskatonic. A philosopher. A widow.

I didn't want to be imprisoned again, trapped inside a corpse, but I inoculated myself from the world. Anything that acutely seduced or repelled me and grasped straight into my heart before, I shoved them away. My heart froze over.

You changed that, Vin. You shattered it apart. Tore apart my gray life and infused it with flowers and strawberry pie. You devastated me in the best way because what I cooled into being wasn't good. You were like magma erupting after the igneous had cooled and everyone thought the volcano went dormant, and they could breathe a sigh of relief that Asenath Waite the firestorm resigned herself to merely exist.

Since November, I've been taken apart and put back together in new ways that have frightened me. In moving past the comfortable life I set up, I've found one more harrowing.

But you're in it. Despite my worst efforts. That's worth everything.

You were, I thought hopelessly, but I might've ruined it. Might've killed you.

And I worry the full metamorphosis might not be able to include you for another set of years. Always transient, never finding a place to settle, never owning a body and home that are eternally mine.

How many ways did I work to discover who I was? I tried to find myself in men's kisses. That rainy day I went to those brothers' house, and I smoked an offered cigarette and casually told them to undress. I knelt and took them in my mouth, and then I let them take turns with me on the bed. One was nervous, so I coaxed my hand across his shoulder as he pushed inside me.

It was fervent and exhausting, and when I laid there and lit another cigarette, a friend of theirs came over. I looked up from the bed, my legs hanging down, and I let him in, too. When I drove home, I bathed and went to bed, not thinking much about it beyond the aching fatigue in my muscles. Thought nothing about whether I was a floozy or what the people back home would think. Didn't keep looking over my shoulder to see if I was being followed. Had dreamless sleeps where I didn't hover over my body as it acted without me.

To me, that was healing. I don't regret what I did, but I've been running in circles. I suppose when one grows up in an environment where tears are forbidden and smiles are suspicious, it cannot be helped that I've taken so long to find what I need.

When I let Dr. Phillips kiss and undress me by the fire, it was different, different for him. He wanted me to be a part of him, part of his life, like his job or his auto. I never wanted to reject him, to break his heart. I only wanted some pleasure; though work offered distraction and a purpose, a routine for my days, and I miss it now, I needed to do things I enjoyed. Go out to eat; visit the cinema; and sleep with someone I was sure wouldn't try to kill me.

Mother, Mother locked in the attic. What would she think if she read this? Deep Ones view sex differently. And grief has different echoes when your people are immortal. I loved her, but I never wanted to be her; rather, I didn't want to be what was done to her.

Because the haze of my mind couldn't separate who I was and what was instinctive based on what others had done. If they mingled so closely together, was there ever a difference? If the universe was merely a set of chemical reactions and eldritch gods who controlled our fates, how could we forge our identities at all?

"Don't ever let them make you feel like nothing," Mother told me in her low croak. "You're the seed of immortal kings and queens." I didn't feel like anything special. Only thin-limbed, feisty Asenath who skipped mathematics to stand idle at the docks. That was special to her. This girl who'd end up with her body stolen and, once she got it back, spent the years trying to make it fit like twisting my hands in a glove again and again.

Vin, you saw something, too. Maybe it was a chance at comfort and security, maybe it was love, but in the end, was there a difference? There in the rising slush of water and earth, I didn't know. Vin, we were both born into this world. Screaming, caked in blood and amniotic fluid. If we were born here, even if there's no intrinsic meaning, doesn't that mean we are meant to be here, allowed to take up space in these bodies we've been given?

I had to find you. Couldn't let you be a casualty of my insecurities. I'd learn, do my best to learn how to help you heal for what time I could stay on land.

A month, a year, I don't know, love, but I'll try.

And, goddamnit, I've lasted this long. If the gods wanted either of us dead, they'd need to come out of the sea and sky, drag their lazy asses here, and kill us themselves.

In that time, dark descended, that pure blackness you won't see in the city at night. I drifted, and then dawn came, and then midday. And as the rain continued, I dragged myself to my knees. Thankfully, my body seemed to absorb and take in the water, and in time, it felt rich as wine, and another burst of nerves and energy overwhelmed, me, so I did the only thing I could do:

With all my might—in a backwards robe soon to be ruined, briars raking their claws down open, salve-greased pustules of blood and slime on my back—

I burst into the heart of the woods.

22. VIN

AFTER I RAN AWAY FROM YOU, I FOUND MYSELF LOST IN THE woods, but truth be told, I wasn't lost at all. That would assume I'd once had a direction I wanted to go in before I went astray.

I was worse. Adrift.

I had no one.

No one in the entire cosmos left. Except, maybe...

I couldn't trust you, and Wilbur, the only other person who ever truly loved me, was dead.

If Papa were alive, he'd only want to use me, and I gave him too much credit. No, he didn't look for me, ever, or if he did, Horror ate him. And Horror was beyond my comprehension. After a point, as he began skulking around Sentinel Hill, feasting on countryside cows, pigs, and goats, I lost the ability to reach him. Quite literally, he became invisible, and despite his massive size, bigger than any barn, I could only know where he was by a ghastly stench with no earthly comparison and the barrel-sized tracks he left in the dirt. Or the mangled dead.

And I was horrified when I saw his visage in the midst of those blue-ringed gray strings that always wriggled, those cobalt and mercury moon-eyes spotting his flesh like moles, that half-face at the center of the slimy mass that was melted and globby as jam, with my purple eyes, my white skin, and my white hair. Papa's eyes, skin, and hair.

And the rest of him, all memories of the thing from beyond that raped me, that took Papa's face and hands, but I saw them both in their horror. Both my rapists, congealed in a monstrous thing that was part-centipede, part-spider, and part-god, like the seed of Pan in old stories.

Godseed, mine, and I flinched away and hid in the house when he grew too big, as if that could protect me.

Alone in the woods with no aim, my mind wandered. A dangerous thing. I thought about home, Papa. How did he feel with me gone? Angry, relieved?

What hurt most about Papa wasn't his cruelty; it was those moments of kindness. When he cooked instead, when he gave me flowers and dolls, even though I was never one for the latter because I feared their stares in the dark. When he carried me home. I caught a glimpse of who he could be, what we could have as father and daughter, the life I might've lived.

And it infuriated me. He played at love, but in the end, he sacrificed Mama, and he wanted to sacrifice me, too. What he did to me in the barn wasn't enough. He gave me crumbs of affection and swept them away.

As the rain soaked me to my core, I wondered if I could plead to the sky and have the gate-and-key come to loop me into its thousands of writhing limbs and make me its true love, make us truly husband and wife with the stars as our witnesses.

It must seem like madness, to desire the monster who possessed Papa and forced me to conceive its offspring. The idea of becoming dust in the stars, whether I'd die or find a transcendental plane of life I couldn't fathom, was what I had left. All along, I wasn't meant for this world, this world of smoke and autos and clambering feet. I was Lavinia of the Whateley family, "those albinos" scattered across the Massachusetts hills between home and Arkham. The ones people detested and whispered about.

As I stiffly jerked through the briars, I found myself in a clearing ringed with poison ivy and wild blackberries. I paused, hands close to my chest. The bear I saw when I came into these woods crept into my mind, its ponderous black eyes.

A familiar stench like death and vomit and softened apples lingered in the air. I recoiled, eyes watering as I covered my mouth. The world spun.

How couldn't I see it before? This was who I was, who I was always meant to be. Multiplying galaxies on my own. That was what the cosmos chose for me, and I'd become too content with being insignificant. Most girls would give any chance to be better, raised from nothing.

Everything around me settled, but though my vision didn't spin, the woods came alive in such a way I can only call unnatural. The branches above me writhed, and I thought it must be the wind, and no, no, I looked up, saw how they eclipsed the stars, and—

My son, the only one left, in the trees. He *was* the trees. He released a low bellow, a wail.

"*Mother,*" he wept.

I gasped, and tears escaped down my cheeks. "Son."

That was the only thing I called him aloud when I'd hold him to me, those few months I could, his sticky tentacles licking my wrist like bile-green tongues and latching his barbed mouths on my nipples to suckle.

By the time they were five years old, Wilbur was a grown man, hunched with a stern brow, always muttering to himself, and Horror couldn't even enter the house. I'd go visit him in the barn when he fit inside, but then he began rampaging the hillsides, always hungry for blood.

I feared, one day, he'd come for mine; he'd tasted it before, when I fed him as he teethed.

Here we were, two lonely creatures meeting in the woods. How could I abandon one of the few things in existence that was a part of me? My own son! Isn't that why mothers exist, to love and care for their children until they die? To neglect him was a terrible reproach on my part. As I looked up into his purple eyes, tears fell from mine.

My poor, poor boy, the only of his kind.

Stars came to life in front of me, and the clearing stirred with light. Novas and flowering natal plants poured themselves in waterfalls around me. I saw their stares in each blackberry eye.

As the wind tangled in my hair and the milk of the universe poured around me, braided itself under my feet, I called to the sky, "*Darkling, I'm listening.*"

The sky answered. Not a sound, but something in the wind, which curled around me. That's the best way I can explain it. What was straight became crooked. No change in smell or sight. At least, not in that second. But the world swelled, convex.

And words slipped into my mind, words I read from a small leather book, words of a woman to another woman, both strict with grief.

Do not urge me to leave you or to turn from following you. For wherever you go, I will go, and wherever you live, I will live. Where you die, I will die, and there I will be buried.

A rustle in the brush behind me. I hoped you didn't try to follow me. You were in no shape—didn't you fall?

I left you there. My stomach twisted into a knot.

You needed me. You hurt me. Both of those were true.

So, what would I do, sacrifice you to the stars, to my son?

You see, what was in the woods didn't speak to me in words. I understood, nonetheless. To be with them, like Papa let the townsfolk feed Mama to the stars, I needed to give you up. Sacrifice you. Let the whip-poor-wills catch your soul with their trills. Only then would I deserve happiness. Be free of pain.

I couldn't bury you.

Couldn't couldn't couldn't.

My trance broke, and horror seeped through. I curled my fists, but when I felt my nails dig into my skin, I stopped.

"No," I whispered.

The world howled back.

No, what am I doing? I thought, the cold crawling back into my elbows. I didn't want to be afraid again. Didn't want to be alone. Wanted to run and keep running to oblivion.

But this wasn't me. No more running.

When I was forced to have the gate-and-key's children, it frightened me. I wasn't in love with that being from beyond the shambling stars. Papa imprisoned me. Abused me. Raped me. Gave me no choices.

I couldn't go back to being a godswife. If I did, I'd die, and something told me that death wouldn't be an easy one. That the promise of eternity wasn't what it seemed. After all, how could I understand what the unknowable gods would do to my body and soul?

It wasn't that I didn't love my sons. My sweet and generous Wilbur, my lonely and beautiful Horror. But I couldn't care for them anymore.

I was alone in the dark woods again. My son must've not been here at all; even invisible, his presence wasn't what one would call subtle. He couldn't merely slip away.

No.

Not that night. Not ever.

I wouldn't die there. Couldn't die there. I was so much more.

I am so much more than what the people in the town thought I was. What Papa thought I was. For so long, I figured if there was an outside consensus of apathy and disgust, they all must be right. Lots more of them than me. But no, they were wrong. I deserved more, and I'd live to see more.

No matter whether I forgave you, I'd live to see you again and help you through your change.

I couldn't tell how long I was there. You said three days, but time seemed to crawl along differently in the dark woods.

After a while of sitting in the cold, it didn't bother me. If I sat there, I could've done it for days. Hopefully, I would've left before I starved.

What did bother me was when you screamed.

23. AZZIE

VIN, I CANNOT BELIEVE WHAT I SAW AND SMELLED WHEN I finally came close to finding you.

The state of things outside was miserable. Water and leaves plastered my body. Because I didn't take the time to change into something more appropriate for walking around in the woods for days, the gown I wore was ruined.

I didn't care about how cold or tired I was. Or the state of my clothes or skin. I only needed to find you. Eventually, nausea and hunger canceled themselves out. I subsisted off adrenaline.

After searching for two more days, everything was a deep black. I was beginning to lose hope.

As miserable as I was, I didn't let myself give up. Not for my sake but for yours.

Noble? I considered why I hid your son's death for you, whether a small and selfish part of me was too tired to frame more of your grief into my life. Hateful. Horrible. Selfish.

I went down another slope, struggling to keep my feet from slipping into the soft ground. Wind rustled through the leaves and carried something repulsive with it. I coughed and choked, saliva thick in my mouth. A horrendous odor traveled along the wind. It was worse than death or decay.

Dead fish, the deer and rabbits and mice I'd come across with their fur and bones half-rotted, half-mummified by the chill.

Worse than those, undoubtedly.

I cannot explain what happened next. I thought I slid against a branch, but what touched me through my clothes wasn't the sharp end of a tree limb. It felt like wet, twitching muscle, and then, something slithered around me, but when I looked around my waist, there was nothing there.

I slapped my hand down on nothing.

Nothing. But. Wetness on my palms. Nothing, not water or blood. Not even a clear fluid. Yet my hand was wet.

The nothing spasmed, kept snaking around me and going tight and loose like menstrual cramps. The stench worsened, and I gagged.

And, before I could try to run, I was lifted off the earth. I struggled, dizzied as I felt a force compress around me, only my fragile flesh keeping it from tapering itself around my ribs.

Your voice: "*No, no, stop! Stop it!*"

And I fell. Not far, only about a foot, but given I'd been raised from the ground by an unknown entity, I had the breath knocked out of me. More than that, the hours upon hours of searching flooded through my veins and caught up with me.

I was sprawled on the mud and leaves, my fin folded painfully under me. The next thing I heard, I. I can't describe it, really. A roar? A scream? It was too human, but absolutely not human. A wail, maybe. And then the horrid stench subsided.

Your face came into view, and I released a sigh of relief. It hurt to breathe.

Even after I drove you to complete, abject misery with my deceit, you leaned down, threw my arm over your shoulder, and helped me stand.

The world kept shuttering around me in the wash of gray, green, and brown.

"I almost did it," you whispered, to me or yourself, "I almost joined him."

The rain had let up hours ago as you guided me miles and miles back.

We said nothing to one another, and I only felt your warmth as I leaned my head against your arm.

Without the rain, I felt weaker until we came across an overflowing pool. The waterfall, which roared.

"I'm already soaked," I said with a laugh. I imagined I must've looked like death if your first instinct was to take me to the water.

You helped me into the stream, and I let myself float in it. I closed my eyes and released deep breaths, trying to rationalize what I witnessed.

A delirium, I told myself, as I trembled and slowly went numb.

When I snapped my eyes open, fearing you left, you were kneeling by the side of the pool, staring at your hands. Where you were, it was partly submerged where the rain had overwhelmed the grass and silt.

We did not speak to each other once as I drifted in the water, feeling the last few strands of my hair falling away. I bet I was no Ophelia. Hell, I didn't have enough hair for petals to fall into.

But I was alive. We are alive.

No matter the odds, we found each other again.

I dared—

I dare myself to hope.

24. AZZIE

THE WALK HOME WAS LONG, MISERABLE, AND SILENT. MY heart swelled like a welt.

Once we got home, wordlessly, you undressed in the washroom, saying nothing as I helped peel your ruined dress off. My own robe was now a rag. You stepped into the bath and turned on the hot water. My senses were so overwhelmed since that strange odor in the woods that my ability to smell was shot. I didn't smell us. We must've been rank.

"It'll be too hot to stand without some cold," I told you. No reply. You stared out as the steaming water rose, and you didn't flinch as the water turned your skin red.

"God, Vin," I said as the water filled half the tub, and I turned the cold on. You looked at me then, but there was nothing in your eyes. I hope I never see you like this again. It was all my fault.

Kneeling to the side of the tub, I set my hand on my arm and pulled away something. A thin, goopy sheet of skin. Scales. My skin was peeling, and scales jutted out from the fin.

Excellent. Just what we both needed.

You only stared ahead, the bottom of your crinkled hair wet. I was beside myself. Afraid you'd given up on me. I deserved it, but I couldn't stand it.

When I saw how the water steamed, how red your skin got, I shut off the faucet once it reached the base of your knees. Candlelight writhed in the water, but it split around you. Your reflection was, too, refracted and broken up.

I muttered, "If I never leave you, please don't leave me again. Please." I was coming from a vulnerable place, more than I'd ever allowed, and we were both selfish in our needs to never be alone, but how could anyone blame either of us? We'd been used for others' selfish desires, so we deserved to treat ourselves even a little.

"Why?" you asked, deathly quiet. Your tangled, leaf-strewn hair was stuck to your cheeks. I looked down and shook my head, but you didn't relent. "When I said I was only a toy, you said that's not all I am. What am I to you?"

My breath caught. "My only friend." My breathing was slow, but a weight lifted off me, like I'd been storing that in my chest like a bear saves its fat for a long winter.

You weren't impressed by that confession. "Friend, is that all?"

"Is that all? Your company, your understanding, that's one of the most precious things you've given me. So yes, you are my friend." I never had any friends, as much as I craved them. And when anyone tried to get familiar, such as Dr. Phillips, I shoved them away.

Your eyes sharply met mine. "Friends don't lie about things like that. You can have your secrets, but not that."

My face crumpled. "I know." I can be awful. Aloof, moody. This was something entirely different. "I lied to you about your son."

Calmly, you explained, "I know you had your reasons, and that those weren't malicious. But it doesn't change what it did to me."

I shook my head. "No, no. Of course not, but that doesn't lessen the impact."

Your voice was miles away, a planet away. "Wilbur's dead. He's dead because I wasn't there to keep him safe. That's what bothers me most."

"Vin, if you had stayed, you'd be dead."

That last word hung in the air. Final. I bowed my head.

You said, "I forgive you."

Snapping up my gaze, my eyes widened so much they ached. Soon enough, I wouldn't be able to shut my eyes at all. "I don't know how you can."

Your lips thinned, eyes haunted. "Neither can I." You turned your head, leaning back and staring forward. We didn't speak for the rest of the day, but when I collapsed into bed, you followed, back to me.

The pistoning of the sewing machine.

"Did you have to make your son's altered clothes? Like this?"

"Yes."

25. Vin

I took to wearing the one black dress I had with faint floral outlines. When you saw me sitting in the recliner with it on, understanding passed between us.

You came and went like a ghost, with the soft creak of your mattress as you slipped into bed. Your wet coughs, I couldn't stand them, couldn't stand ignoring your pain. Your scales were beautiful, but the cost...

My son was dead.

Wilbur was. Is. Horror, I don't know. Maybe he died, too, alone and abandoned in the woods. Died and joined his father. The gate-and-key. Yog-Sothoth. How absurd it all was. Papa was so determined to have his half-god grandchildren, demigods, maybe so he could say that he did, but there was no grand prophecy.

Demigods, it turns out, were as disposable as me.

Maybe that was for the best, I thought bitterly. The stars don't mourn, and I was never meant to have a family.

After my time in the woods, though, I knew I'd never join them up there. I can't leap from a passing nightmare to an eternal one. Those worlds inside worlds and galaxies Papa fawned over and sought to explore weren't what I wanted. Not when I knew so little about this world, the people and restaurants and films and grand sights I'd only read about.

Spending decades pining over far-off abysses always felt foolish to me. Let me know and love my world first.

Standing, fists curled in my sides, I passed the door frame, as I had what must've been hundred of times, and I stopped when I saw you. Your pale head as you cocooned yourself in your sheets right in the middle of the bed. You were so tiny and shriveled in the salt-streaked expanse of your bed. When I went to your side and set a hand to your brow, your forehead was burning.

I wasn't Papa; I couldn't ignore suffering.

Heading to the washroom, I took a cloth and wet it with our stash of closed buckets of water, since the pipes were frozen. Though it was spring, the temperature sometimes dipped at night, and the pipes froze until late evening.

Silently, I came in and reached to press the cloth against the dull sheen of your brow. Mucus was wet above your lips.

"Thank you," you murmured, eyes fluttering open. "I feel wretched."

"I know," I said. All I could think to say.

When you drifted from me in a shallow sleep, I traced a line across the back of your hand with my thumb.

I couldn't deny that I continued to want to be with you. We didn't understand each other's methods of coping, but that could be learned. All we needed was time, which was in short supply.

I wrung out the cloth in the sink and set it on the porcelain, deciding to check on the garden. When I went outside, the boards below my slippers creaked from the dampness. I had half a mind to swing my body lazily in the hammock before tending to anything.

A black auto pulled up close to the strawberries. Not expecting the incursion, my fingers buried themselves in the porch railing.

A man stepped out, wearing an immaculate gray suit and a smart white hat. Without any doubt, he approached me, brow raised in a question; if only I could have his confidence, to walk toward a stranger without fear of violence. I try more nowadays. But it's hard.

"Ah, hello," he said with a perfunctory smile. "You look much better." He stopped a foot from the steps.

Surliness riled in me, pooled in my taut shoulders. I never asked him how I looked. Yet so many people throughout my life needed to give me their opinion. Chin too small. Skin too pale. Eyes too void. I kept my voice politely calm, but it was difficult to smile during those long days. "Hello. I'm not sure we've met."

He removed his boater hat and rotated it with both hands before him. Conciliatory. "Forgive me. I'm Dr. John Phillips."

Your physician. I don't think I ever saw him, but he recognized me. Granted, I wasn't what you'd call an inconspicuous person. "You. Uh. Did you see me when I first came here?"

He bowed his head in acknowledgement. His face and nascent beard were well-groomed. Dr. Phillips was a handsome man, but there was something stiff about his movements and expressions. Suppose he could've said the same about me. "Yes, as a matter of fact. You were terribly burned from the sunlight."

My hand fell to my elbow. "I have an ointment for it now."

"That's good."

After a pause, I asked him, "May I ask why we have the pleasure of you calling on us?"

He tucked his hat under his arm. "I was coming to see how Asenath was faring. She hasn't called or visited me in months. Is she in?"

"She's out at the moment." He glanced at your auto, and so did I. "Taking a stroll in the woods."

He peered to his right, as if he'd see you coming around one of the trees. "When do you think she'll return?"

"I'm not sure. She didn't say."

"Are you absolutely sure she isn't here? I swore I saw someone in the window."

"No, she isn't. I'm terribly sorry, sir."

He stared, as if the words were catching up to him. "Ah, I see. Well, sorry to bother you. I'll be on my way." He went to go and pointed his hat to the golden daffodils. "They are coming along quite well."

"Wait." He stopped. A hand went to my hair, worrying it. "I think she might need more laudanum."

"Oh dear." He settled his hat back on his combed brown hair. "Still having sleep troubles?"

"Yes," I said.

He gave me a tincture of it from his suitcase. I didn't move until I saw the auto drive away, and I told myself I imagined the scowl on his face, the phantom of suspicion.

After, I went to you.

You drowsily snapped open one eye. "Hm, were you talking to someone?"

I sat by you. "Yes, Dr. Phillips."

Scowling, you sat up on your side, and I handed you the tincture. We shared a look.

You shook your head. "He's harmless. Annoyingly persistent, but harmless."

I frowned. "Being polite isn't the same as harmless."

You eased deeper into your pillow and sighed. "True enough."

"He did seem persistent. Didn't you say he pined after you?"

You rested down again in silence, and I believed that you fell asleep with your eyes open, which you'd been doing for a few nights, until you spoke again. "I slept with him, and he thought he loved me."

"Did you love him?" I asked.

You dropped your eyes and shook your head. Your chest rose, a sigh withheld. "No. I did feel guilty. When I rejected him, he seemed wounded."

"If you didn't want him, accepting his advances would've hurt both of you in the long run."

A haunted shadow crept into your eyes. "You're always generous in your idea of me, even after what I've done. How did Dr. Phillips make you feel?"

"Indifferent," I replied, the truth. "And I don't see it as generous. Just normal."

You achingly smiled, lips chapped, eyelids heavy but straining against your swollen eyes. "Normal, hm." I stayed by your side as you drifted, the glass bottle pressed to your chest, and I couldn't shake the unease curdling in the hollow of my stomach.

26. AZZIE

ONCE THE ~~MERMBRANES~~ MEMBRANES BETWEEN MY FINGERS and toes began to form, slime came with them.

Splendid.

Now, it takes me twice as long to type. I must look ridiculous, fumbling over the keys like this, doing everything one key at a time.

I raised my hand to the bedroom window, looking at it in the soft, golden sunlight which made the dust particles into little stars. I could see through the greenish membranes, though veins were starting to form.

Last week, the edges of my eyes grew jaundiced and horrible. The new scales on my back, spreading from my fin, were scintillating and shuddered between green and blue.

When I look in the mirror, I almost convince myself I can love them, these beautiful colors on an inbetween thing like me. This spectacular miracle from only my part of the world.

Thankfully, the ~~piopes~~ pipes were no longer frozen, so I could bathe. Sometimes, I stayed in the tub for three hours. The cooled water didn't bother me. You came to collect dirty towels off the tiles.

I said to you, "I'm not sure if you should touch me. What if I'm poisonous?"

You blinked. "Venomous."

I drawled, "Yes, that."

"May I try?" you asked.

I wanted to give an emphatic yes, Vin, but I was scared and falling deeper into a dark, cramped cavity in the bleak and unforgiving sea. "If you want."

"I can't believe with all this, I haven't grown a few inches. I expected to be more imposing. Dangerous."

A free hand on my shoulder, you said, "Maybe one day. Though you did scare the soul out of that man outside the theater." Scare the soul out. Interesting choice of words.

I tilted my head to the side. "It always seems to be something. Wanting to be taller, curvier. Everything."

"Have you always felt this way?" you asked me, and I caught a sadness in your voice. I thought to myself, as I had many times before: How can I tell her the truth without saying it?

"No. I feel like my body doesn't belong to me. For so long, it belonged to Father. He controlled everything."

I didn't lie. In fact, I told you the blunt truth, so why do I feel guilty? You'd offered so much of yourself to me at risk of judgment and abandonment.

You waved a hand toward my fin. "Does he control this? Has he ever seen you like this?"

"No, but I still didn't choose this." Another decision taken away from me. The only choice left was to let the pain fester and be prolonged on land or go into the sea.

Your smile was sad. "I know. Do you think you could ever love your body like this, like I love it?"

I thought about your question. "It's different." The mirror of my mind is milky, glossed over.

"Different," you repeated.

Unlike with any other person, I took quite some time to reply to you with anything substantive. I liked that. I liked that, with no judgment, you waited until I was ready. "You liked me before the change, and I. I. I don't know how I feel about myself. And even now, you see the ghost of what I was. By the time I've fully changed—monster teeth, all scales and slime and fins, I don't know if you could. And I wouldn't blame you."

After the bath, there I sat on my bed, miserable and agonizing over my changing body. My skin absorbed the water, but I was still damp. All my life, the parts of it I remembered, I worked to be beautiful. Specific types. What Father thought I should be, until I couldn't tell whether I was working to please myself, Father, society or a mix of all three.

And with my change into a Deep One, all that went out into the bin. Because the Deep Ones are entirely different; that side of my heritage was occluded at home, despite my town worshiping Father Dagon and Mother Hydra. The city in the depths, Y'ha-nthlei, was one of hundreds of homes of the Deep Ones, and those were only the cities for those people. Thousands of different beings thrived at the bottom of the ocean, and some even whispered about Old Ones sleeping there. Beings beyond comprehension, waiting to wake while infesting mortal dreams with their incomprehensible visions.

So, in working terribly long to understand my body, it soon became unknown to me. And what I felt was strange repulsed me; I was withering. Hideous.

And that was when you sidled by my side, our bare feet on the floor, and took my webbed hand into yours. With you so close, I smelled rose milk soap, the one that was easier on your skin, and on mine.

You pressed a kiss to the tip of my forefinger, and your soft lips lingered there until your tongue poked out. I sucked in a deep breath and let you take my finger into your mouth. In the paltry three years since I came back into myself at age twenty-five, I'd let men, and a few women, do many things to my body. My constant battle to reclaim my autonomy, to decide what I liked for myself.

But never do I think I ever so swiftly grew rapt and felt that tell-tale pang below my navel than when you teased my finger and, holding my hand firm, reached up and gently stroked one of the thin membranes. A jolt of pleasure came from that sensitive stretch of flesh, and I released a helpless moan.

You stopped far too soon, and asked me, "Did that feel good?"

"Yeah," I said, failing to compose myself under your curious and mischievous stare. "Touch it, touch that part again. I've never..." You did, mirroring your hand against mine and bending your thumb to slide it across that paper-thin web of skin.

I sweated profusely, and the skin around my neck and back were peeling and disgusted me. And yet, you made me positively vibrate under your touch, driven mad by need. It was enough to make me forget that I'd decided I must be undesirable, unfit for human eyes.

You leaned in, and you flicked your tongue against the membrane, and I gasped. My legs impatiently moved, my knees inward. I needed to lie down, I needed your lips on me; I needed every part of you to consume me and take me away from the reality of my frail, molting body.

No longer was I shriveling away like a summer flower in winter. Under your tender control, my pleasure multiplied, a mitosis between us.

With achingly painful slowness, you kissed each of my fingertips as you caressed the membranes between them. Never had I thought a mere touch of my hands would threaten to dissolve me into a mess of moans. I was ready to beg. Part of me considered this was a punishment for my past mistakes.

"Vin," I whispered.

"Hm?" you asked, hot lips against my palm, kissing the hard, scaly skin where I'd broken the vodka glass.

"I need you," I said, meaning it desperately. All the emotions I had when you left collided into me, my heart slamming into my ribs. My throat ached.

"Oh." You perked up, grinning. "I'm here." As I reflect, this side of you is rare, but it's one I love the most, that cheekiness. I was ready to let you do anything to me.

"Here," I said, touching your knee, thumb brushing against some of the fragile white hairs on your legs. As needy as I was, I decided I should reciprocate. "Lie back on the pillows."

"You know," you whispered with my hand to your cheek, breath on my neck. "I quite like this arrangement. I'm not sure I want to give it up." Your tongue moved to the side of your mouth.

"You won't need to," I replied shakily.

We broke apart, and you set your shoulders on the pillow, so you were half-sitting, half-lying in the middle of the bed. I shifted, so we observed each other through partly lidded gazes. As I reached to feel the velvet of your blue dress, I thought I'd like this to last forever, to get lost counting each of your silver eyelashes.

Since my fin came in, my movements were slower and stiffer. Carefully, I twisted, setting a single knee farther on the bed. My bones popped and creaked, as if I were old, and your hand gripped my elbow to steady me as I fully knelt next to you.

My webbed hand now fell to that vortex of fabric pooled at your thighs. The corners of your mouth deepened as I slowly lifted up the hem of your dress, revealing cream-colored, striped bloomers with lace circling each of your legs.

I teased, "Do I have your permission to remove these, Your Highness?"

You tilted your head. "Is that what we're playing here?"

"If you wish," I replied. I could always pretend you were Mother Hydra, Queen of the Sea.

Righting your head, you tilted your chin and said, "Yes."

With that, I touched the waistband, which left a small indent in your skin, and let my fingers gloss over the sensitive skin there. You shifted, eyes a little more open, as I took my time to grip the bloomers down and work them past your knees, your finely shaped ankles, and your toes. With them set on the sheets, I had a good sight of your gash, which was glistening a little underneath a curly patch of hair.

I moved to get between your legs, and you helpfully widened the space between them, so I could fit, kneeling before you on my hands and knees. By now, my gown clung to my breasts and armpits with all the sweat and slime of me, but I no longer cared, no longer mired myself in shame. You'd given me a task to focus on.

Bending my head, I deliberated on what to do; before you, it'd been a while since I'd been with a woman. Instead of going straight to pleasuring you, I pressed a fluttering kiss to the inside of your left knee, which you'd raised. I only caught a glimpse of your expression, but my heart tensed at how soft it was.

I continued to kiss your soft skin, from your knees to the pale stretch marks on the inside of your knee, leading to the center of your wet need. Only then, did I offer a kiss to your pubic bone and a brief lick to your clit. You jumped, one of your hands twisting in the sheets, and another lifting to grasp the end of the pillow.

With a smirk, I lowered my head and licked loose circles around your clit, inching my fingers close to the base of your slit and sliding one in. Your breaths grew more troubled as my touches deepened, and my finger slid in more, joined with another. I moved my tongue down to trace the whole of you, and I delighted in the sweet mildness of your taste.

As I continued my work, the room dimmed as rain thrummed against the room, and once you tensed, I could tell you were close, about to spill over. Just then, I pulled back and sat on my haunches.

I contemplated what to do next or whether to continue, and you said, "I want to make you happy, too."

While you kept your dress on, only hitched up, you helped me out of mine, which was made easier with the gap in the back for my fin. Setting your hand on my shoulder blade, you traced a line across the new rash of scales pebbling the skin.

Leaning in, you kissed me there, knuckles grazing against my fin, and I found that the sensation was as sensitive as touching that space behind my knee or my naked spine. My old spine, that fin and scales. Destroyed and remade, sharp and slippery and not entirely mine.

At least, didn't feel like it yet. Those brief touches toyed with me, had me hanging on to your every ministration. I wasn't sure how much of that was deliberate or in the five months we'd known one another, you'd begun to understand the language of my body.

When your lips stopped grazing against my scales, and you pulled back, I felt a loss. Responding to your silent instructions, I moved to the warm spot where you'd been, but I paused.

"You don't need to," I said.

You paused. "All right."

"I'm having that time of the month," I explained.

Your look was full of mirth. "That's okay. It's not like I haven't seen blood."

"My blood included," I said dryly, deliberating on what to do next.

"Yes, that."

"I was thinking..." I pursed my lips, unsure how to explain it. You leaned, listening. I inched forward, so we were side by side, and patted the spot by your right knee. "Here, lie on your side. With your feet near the pillows."

With a small grin, you did as I instructed, hair strewn near the footboard. The ease in your movements was a world away from how hunched and reticent you were the day we met.

Much more slowly, I did the mirror inverse of you, lying on my side, so I could stroke where your thighs met the hair below your navel. Intuiting what I was going to do, you further moved your top leg back.

I brushed my palm against your hip and reached between your lips to stroke your clit, my palm pressing on it as my fingers went to your slit. You, too, began to tease mine, albeit more tentatively, since you were still new to these kinds of pleasures.

Craning my neck to taste you hurt more than it once did; my completely changed spined made the relationship my nerves had with themselves volatile. Nevertheless, my tongue found your clit, and my fingers worked in you as you returned the favor.

The pleasure you gave me, dovetailed with tasting your sweet musk, brought me close as your hands trailed my outer leg. My body was fully rapt, nipples stiff and breasts flush with gooseflesh.

You came first, reaching your climax with soft gasps against my sensitive part. You shuddered, and I soon found myself spilling over, too, tasting the mild but dulce salt of your arousal.

Our limbs and mouths tangled in each other, it was all I could ever dream of.

Once we were done, we moved so we rested with both our heads on the pillows. While I was naked, you still had on your dress.

You trailed your finger along the side of the fin with a kiss pressed to my shoulder. I closed myself and thanked whoever would listen that we were still here, that we could have this moment of peace.

I barely think of myself as Asenath Waite, daughter of Ephraim and

Penelope Waite, anymore. Peering through the glass darkly, I think of myself as Azzie, a name you gave me.

"You're like a pearl to me," you said.

"Thank you," was all I managed to say at first, throat thick with emotion. Funny, I'd always thought the same about you. I became a little melancholy as the adrenaline faded. "But pearls get washed away." That wasn't entirely true; pearls didn't belong on land in the first place.

"Pearls can wash back up, too," you said faintly.

I let that calm me further. "Indeed, they can." Foreheads together, we fell asleep, though sometime in our doze you woke up and left for the mail. When I groggily stirred, you were saying my name with the newspaper clutch tight in your left hand.

"Asenath," you said, tone grave. When my complete first name escaped your lips, I knew it couldn't be good, but I underestimated the dire news you'd give me, the kind that can crush anyone's spirit.

As I sat up, tense, you handed me the paper, giving me the courtesy I didn't give you, these shared breaths that melt into tears. I read it.

Isolated Massachusetts Hamlet Raided by Federal Forces
    By Wingate Peaslee
    April 15, 1933

Federal forces, under an executive order from President Roosevelt, raided the seaside Massachusetts town of Innsmouth early Tuesday morning. The reasons for the raid are unknown, though there are reports that a whistle-blower intimated foul wrongdoings in the town.

On the heels of discussions for an amendment to abolish the prohibition of alcohol, sources from the neighboring town of Newburyport have cited rampant illegal trading in the area, though the President promised no prosecutions for the buying and selling of alcohol.

The coral reefs surrounding the town's harbor were obliterated by multiple bombings conducted with federal supervision. All suspicious persons were arrested and taken into custody. No reasons were disclosed.

There is no word on their fate or if there will be a trial for undisclosed wrongdoing. A rumor persists that these individuals exhibited strange behavior and deformations, and to keep the general populace safe, they are being kept at specialized detainment facilities for an indefinite amount of time.

Innsmouth, surrounded by inhospitable salt marshes, was once a bustling sea port but has fallen on hard times since before the 1929 stock market crash; the War of 1812 proved fatal to its many ship-building enterprises, leaving the town's only notable qualities to be its extensive ship graveyard and the forever present odor of dead fish. It is noted that census reports for the town are outdated, with the latest number up to 1,856 in 1923, because all newcomers to the town were treated with immediate hostility. The full number of arrests is unknown but is speculated to be around 900 residents.

The investigation into what happened in the obscure hamlet remains ongoing.

My town was found out.

My people were taken.

And Mother...

I clutched the paper to my chest, heart in my throat. "Mother went to the reef. Mother ..."

Never before did I let you see me cry, and truth be told, I never felt the urge to weep, except for when I experienced the mind-twisting pain of my transformation.

Never, but. I crumbled.

My sobs came out violently from deep in my chest.

I was naked, crumbling into myself, a sticky mess of slime and sweat and blood. You wrapped your arms around me and pulled me into you, letting me spill my tears against the teal of your dress.

I can't help but feel it was a comeuppance, a forced equilibrium.

"I did this," I muttered, nonsensical and inconsolable. If I blamed myself for something out of my depths, I could pretend I had control of my spiraling life. "I can't breathe, I can't do it, I want to die, Vin, I can't do it anymore..."

"No," you murmured against my brow. "No, no, no."

Your touch and words lulled me into sleep, or rather, my body shut down and left me in the realm of dark and thorned nightmares.

27. VIN

GRIEF FINDS WAYS TO SOFTEN AND HARDEN, SO WE NO LONGER recognize the terrain of our minds. We were numb and angry and tired at once. How one could be numb yet full of a hundred emotions, I never understood. A darkness lurked in me, and I despised it; I never wanted the world to turn me to stone.

Together, we were insatiable, and perhaps that was my saving grace.

One rainy morning, I found you bent over and kneeling on the floor, on all fours, eating a half-frozen pie you must've taken out of the icebox. With your webbed fingers, you dipped your hand into the globby, congealed red mire and smeared the crumbs and filling on your pale lips. You'd taken a cup of salt and poured it in the red wound of the strawberry pie, so it formed a crust like a moon dune around the edge that you scraped with your fingers and teeth.

Myself, I couldn't bring myself to eat much, but I was happy that for a brief while, you could stomach food. In fact, you were ravenous. What I did take in were those times you came to me and shucked off your nightgown. You did that then, standing with the crumbs scattered on the floor, and I helped you. The slitted fabric around your fin ripped, but we didn't care.

I drank in your messy strawberry kiss, licked your sweat, your saline.

Let myself be lost in your embrace. Feeling your passionate lips against my neck, my breasts, my hip, having that desperation for love and acceptance and escape roll in waves off her, it smoothed my edges, softened me again, as if you patted slip against my cracked bones.

And when you started biting, I let you.

When you looked at me in apology, I told you that I wanted more.

After you tried to hide Wilbur's death, I contemplated sleeping in the guest bedroom again, so in tumult, but thinking about it after you learned about your town's ruination only brought guilt.

We were both alone, except for each other.

In bed, when I pulled my hand away from your cheek, dead skin coated my palm, trails of mucus following.

"The rest of it," is all you said, tiredly reaching toward your hip, and I understood; your fin was growing again and filling out the lower part of your back.

I can't describe the sound of your bones rearranging and muscles stretching inside you; the best I can relate it to is how the porch steps wetly creak after a storm.

"You're taller than me now," I teased.

"Yes," you murmured, adding wryly, "I now know what it's like you be the tallest in a pair."

Some times were less easy. When you'd sob in agony.

All I could do was touch your shoulder. "I'm sorry. I'm sorry. I don't know what to do."

"Be with me." The two of us, alone in the world.

When I helped you up out of bed, you grimaced and couldn't fully stand, so you hunched over as I helped you into the warm, salty bath.

"Do you need the laudanum?" You had begun rationing the newest bottle.

You laughed without mirth. "I think we're well past the opium helping."

"You're addicted to it. If you don't take it..." I didn't know what'd happen.

Blearily, you said, "Vin, I don't honestly think it'll cause me more pain than I'm already in."

"Would you be better off in the ocean? Would that be less painful?"

The look you gave me sent chills down me. No anger or annoyance. Only haunted. "Let's not discuss that. I don't want to argue."

We keep dancing around things to keep from hurting each other, but we end up stepping on each other's tails.

It's hard not to when we never talk about what's bothering us. We're bound to step on what we don't see.

"Your mother might still be alive."

"Don't. Don't talk about her, please."

To make you have hope was cruel of me.

28. Azzie

I cannot stop shaking. I still cannot believe what I've done. And that you, without protest, helped me cover it up. I feel dangerous and sick and alive all at once.

You slept by my side, farthest from the window, facing me. I noticed how often you let your back face the wall, as if you feared something from the woods would steal you away. The woods, or elsewhere.

A creak in the porch broke me from sleep for a second. My vision blurred, but I saw nothing but the flickering lamp on the nightstand behind your head. I wished I could roll over on my back.

The cottage wasn't too old, but it groaned in the night, so I thought nothing of the occasional noises. Especially when it rained, a cacophony kept me up the first week I was here, hypervigilant as I was.

Any second, I thought Father would come to my front door or stand at my bedroom window in whatever new body he acquired. His eyes would fall on me, and I'd turned to ice.

My eyesight flickered in and out from exhaustion.

A light flared before me in the dark of the room. I went stone-still.

Dr. Phillips was standing at the end of my bed, holding a lantern up to take in my appearance. My lack of hair, my gills, my scales.

In his pale blue eyes, in the firelight there, I saw myself, and I caught the absolute, undiluted fear rippling through him. Fear which turned to piteous revulsion. It hurt me. For so long I tried to accept my body, to find it beautiful by seeking the approval of others, of men and women who'd find it desirable.

"Asenath, what happened to you?"

He was the hero, coming to save me from an intruder. That day he came and only saw Vin standing outside and being too standoffish for his liking. In his mind, she shifted from cool to uncivil to dangerous.

I shifted so my feet faced the edge of the bed, so I could run and attack him if need be. With that, he caught a glimpse of my fin, pupils dilating in a sea of white.

"God, what is that?" he asked. I didn't answer.

Vin stirred. When she turned her head to see Dr. Phillips standing there, she froze.

"We can talk about this," I told him, holding up my hands. I didn't think I needed to fear the mild-mannered doctor, but an odd lightning danced in his eyes. I was reminded of my father whenever he came across a scientific curiosity or theory he wanted to dissect.

The last thing I needed Dr. Phillips to do was leak this to anyone. The authorities. The press. With the discovery of my home, the "deformities," Dr. Phillips might not know the nature of what I am, but those with much more power to corral me might. And, for as long as I live, I won't ever let myself be culled. Never again.

And then, from the inside of his coat, he pulled out a revolver and aimed it at you. And my mind turned. Soured. Enough worrying over my fate.

I reached out both my hands, forgetting that showing him the membranes between my fingers might not endear him to the image of me. "John, stop."

Voice high and hollow, he asked you, "What did you do to her?"

"W-what do you mean?" you asked, shoulders tensed, voice still groggy from interrupted sleep.

Perhaps, aligning with the superstitions embedded in the soil, he thought you were a witch. That did seem like the assumption a more close-minded person might make.

His eyes narrowed to slits. Behind his thick lenses, He looked like a wolf on the hunt.

I slipped out of bed, leaning with my hand against the mattress, preparing to knock him off balance. "If you hurt her, I swear it'll be the last thing you do."

I wanted to rip open his throat, hear his bones crack under my teeth.

He shot a round, then, right into my headboard, an inch from your face. You yelped, both hands over your mouth.

Unthinking and uncaring, I lunged at him. I swept forward like the tide and knocked right into his side with that strength that'd been churning in me, that immortal blood of underwater kings and queens.

I'm so terribly hungry.

I was so terribly hungry.

This bastard wanted to be inside me so terribly, but he was inconsiderate. He never considered that I wanted to put my teeth inside him.

I was so goddamned hungry, and he was going to feed me.

With a pained intake of breath, he fell backwards, and his head slammed into the corner of the dresser. His skull sickly cracked, and after a violent jerk, he went still as he collapsed on the floor. His glasses fell on the floor, one lens popping out of its frame and siding under the bed.

My saliva throbbed in my mouth, and then I could feel his pulse fade through my own body, my feet feeling the tremors his body made before he went slack. Your labored breaths filled the room, as did the smells of blood and gunsmoke.

He was dead. Because of me. I killed him. Breathing was a struggle; it was knocked right out of me.

I don't remember how I got to be above him. I think I crawled to the floor. The world was a blur. I heard your voice, but instead of answering, I opened my mouth, and I dug my teeth into the tender flesh of his neck, still warm as his metallic taste flooded me. I used my clumsy fins to shovel his flesh, his vocal folds, his windpipe all into my open mouth, which suddenly felt much wider.

Finally, I was getting full again.

"Azzie."

When I looked at you, you clasped your hands to your chest, silent tears cascading down your cheeks.

With your knees, you moved across the bed, and for that taut and unknowable second, you reached out, and we twined our fingers together.

29. Vin

For a long time, we stood together above the body, which leaked. Your breaths were heavy and bubbled with phlegm and blood. Before I said a word, your eyes flickered with a forming plan. As if this weren't your first time planning how to dispose of a body.

Horror or no, the surprises never ceased.

You went into your closet and produced long, thin, moth-eaten blankets that were a muted ice-blue. Like the one you gave me after a nightmare. Blankets and opium, your love language. Opium, was that what made your eyes bloodshot and pupils small?

You set the blankets on the ground before the back door. Together, we rolled him in one and used the other to carry him out the back door. Difficult work, going out the back door, with me holding his head and you his feet.

To guide him out, we both lifted the bottom fabric. My shoulders went tense, a pain radiating from them to my wrist. At first, I thought you planned to set his body on fire in the burn pile. Seeing the ashened, rain-scattered papers in the pit made a lump form in my throat.

Dawn bathed the world in a lighter blue. My mind was a flurry. I didn't want the doctor dead, but my heart was still in my throat from when he pointed his gun at me.

Instead of dropping him in the ashes, you guided me to the woods, down a generous slope. As we went, my blood went cold when I caught a scrap of deep purple in one of the birch hollows.

Not like my eyes or that one dress I have. Dark, like Papa's robes. Yes, that exact color. I blinked, and yes, it was still there. An errant cloth, and if I looked close enough, which was difficult as we moved a body, I swore I saw the tail-end of a constellation. Papa's special robes had the night sky on them.

And then my vision flashed, and I saw him there on the ground, his eyes gaping red chasms where the crows plucked them clean. I'd reach out, and would I leave him? Bury him? Slam my fists into his chest and spit in his face? I couldn't say. I liked to think one of my sons killed him after I left. I wasn't sure which was better. Wilbur driving an ax through his skull or Horror devouring him.

As soon as I imagined him, he was gone, leaving only that expanse of newly sprouted weeds and wildflowers over the old, dead leaves.

Would Papa ever look for me, only to get lost and die out here? No. That'd give him too much credit. In the end, he got what he wanted from me. Missing, dead. He never cared.

But would he look for my last son, if he were around here?

I was going mad. Between seeing Horror or thinking I did, thinking I saw him try to hurt you—the world was askew, unright.

We went far, which we couldn't have done without your new strength, until you set his feet down on the earth. Leaning to the side, you released squelching gasps, coughing up phlegm and spitting it out alongside globs of blood. I set down Dr. Phillips' head, barely attached to the remaining strings of his throat and hanging out of the blanket, as gently as possible and went to stand by you. You cleared your throat.

"I need to go get a shovel," you said to me. "Are you okay staying here? Or do you want to go back with me?"

I pursed my lips together and considered it. "I can stay here." Though he tried to shoot me, I pitied Phillips. His paranoia, his jealousy, none of that meant his body should rest above ground alone.

You gave a little nod, and when you went back, I was surprised at how agile you were. I half-expected, with how you hunched closer to the ground, that you'd begin running on all fours like I read the Deep Ones did in Papa's books about the worshipers of Dagon and Hydra. You didn't.

Without incident, you returned with a shovel in your hand, and you struck the soil.

I reached out a hand. "Are you sure you can do this?"

These days were confusing for both of us, how you swung from horribly fatigued and in pain to full of energy and strength. In the latter days, you would also be more eager to kiss and play in bed with me, but you'd get far more irritated than usual if the coffee maker acted up or the pipes froze and began muttering curses under your breath. *Oh, of course you did that, you goddamn stupid thing.*

Such as now, when you realized that the loam, clay and silt, hardened with the coolness of day, took some effort to give way. "Goddamn it, you rusty piece of shit." You snapped up your head and tilted it in bemusement. "Sorry, did you say something?"

I pointed toward the shovel. "Are you sure you can do this? I could get one of the garden spades and help, if you need."

"Yes." You were already out of breath, but you didn't sound tired. In fact, blood-smeared as you were, your eyes were clearer than they'd been in a month. "Yes, this is my fault. I should bury him, at least." As you cast your gaze from the shrouded body to the shovel, an iron resolve darkened your eyes. "I can do this."

Giving you a nod, I sat by the nearest birch, near a ring of dandelions, and let you work. I couldn't dare to relax, but I leaned against the coarse bark.

As you worked, the sun rose and granted us more light. Each twitch of the trees, every silhouette that moved, distracted me. Surviving this long made me overly paranoid, but what we were doing was decidedly outside the law.

Softly, as you dug, you hummed under your breath.

"His auto," I murmured, wringing my hands. "His auto must be parked somewhere."

"I didn't hear him pull up or come in. He must've parked at a distance to conceal himself." You paused. You had about a foot of earth heaved in a small mound. "I'll check later." You resumed humming as you continued the bitter work.

"What's that song?" I asked you. "The one you were humming."

"Oh, some sea shanty the sailors on the docks used to sing when I was smoking. Something about a dead horse."

"Were the men ever bothered that there was a young girl smoking on the harbor?"

Meeting my eyes, your mouth lifted in a sad smile. "No, they never bothered me. And there weren't many of them after the nineteenth-century. Mostly goods like cigars."

A lapse of silence, and then you began to sing: "*We'll use the hair of his tail to sew our sails. And the iron of his shoe to make deck nails. We'll hoist him up to the fore yard-arm where he won't do sailors any harm. We'll drop him down with a long, long roll. Where the sharks will have his body, and the Devil'll take his soul.*"

Tremulously, throat hoarse, I sang with you until Dr. Phillips, the poor soul, was buried. I helped you put his body in the grave and watched as you put the soil over him. With a great heave, you leaned against the shovel. With a deep breath, you dropped it and came to sit across from me.

Dr. Phillips was laid to rest. I didn't send a prayer to the gods, as I didn't know if they listened, and if they listened, well, I preferred being discreet.

The silence hung heavy. Anything might've eased it.

You murmured, "He isn't the first man I've killed."

Not that, evidently.

I took that in. Wilbur's death. Your town's fate. Whether your mother was alive. Too much. Numbness lingered. It'd take years for it to subside a little.

Maybe that should've frightened me, that you were capable of such violence against those who threatened you and those you loved. No small reveal.

When I lived over thirty years of my life with Papa, who talked about sacrificing me to a pyre, and the songbirds crept along the branches to steal souls, I was nonplussed.

Besides that, it felt good to be worth protecting.

"Who were the others?" I asked.

You ran a hand over your face, looking as if you'd aged decades in these past few hours. "There was only one other. Intentional, anyway." You didn't answer, but your father came to mind with how nonchalantly you spoke about his death. Good riddance.

"Did he do something?" Not an inquiry I'd give most people who admitted to murder.

"Yes," you replied fiercely, and I caught a glimpse of your glassy, long fish-teeth. "No one deserved it more than him. I shot him six goddamn times for what he did." You stared at Dr. Phillips' shrouded body. "He didn't. He didn't, and I killed him."

"It was an accident," I said. It was weak, but it was all I had. The world was a mad one, askew, unfair, nonsensical, but this moment in particular felt like everything tumbled to a slant.

You set your hands in your lap. "The result's the same. And to be truthful, I'm not sure it was an accident."

With my knuckles on my brow, I brushed back the hair from my face. "What do you mean? You lost control. That's all."

"He was pointing that gun at you, and my mind went blank. I wanted to sink my teeth into him, dig them into his neck, taste his blood. Nothing has ever made me angrier, not even...not even what Father did." Though you alluded to your father's crimes, I never pried. Like you let me kiss you when I was ready, I'd wait despite our rapidly shortening time.

I wasn't sure how to feel, hearing this admission while I sat by the grave of a man my partner killed. No one in the past had threatened another soul to defend me.

I remembered when we stood outside the Cimarron in November, which felt like ages ago. How you brightly told a man you'd remove his hand if he touched my hair without my consent again. I couldn't deny that having someone go feral for me, to protect me, it aroused me.

In the end, though, I didn't want anyone to die. There'd been enough pain and bloodshed.

You sucked in a long breath. "I think I must be a monster. We spend our lives denying it, hiding it. No one wants to be a monster, but what if all this time I've worked to conceal myself when I should just accept it?"

I swallowed thickly. "Depends on what you mean by 'monster'. Most people see anything that's different as a monster. A lot of people probably think I'm one." Of all the literature I've read, the only people who looked like me were villains. These sly, white-haired, red-eyed devils. Rather than people whose skin burned easily and whose eyesight could be touchy at best.

With a huff, you said, "That's because they need to find someone to hate for a spurious reason."

"You're only different now. Not a monster." And if you were a monster, you were my protector. My lighthouse.

"My father was human, and he did unspeakable things to me. Most people are distant and absorbed in their own lives. My mother was the only one who looked at me and saw Asenath. Her, and then you. But as for the rest of the humans, I'm starting to think being a monster to all of them isn't that terrible. At least, it doesn't speak terribly of me."

"As long as it makes you happy," I said. I meant it.

Monster, human, I'd learned the lines were blurred long ago. And indeed, if my sons were monsters, they'd been the kindest to me. Even Horror, I knew, even with that insatiable need to devour everything, loved me. Loved me as he could, a poor child forced into Papa's cosmic schemes.

Our eyes met, and I saw it all: your sadness, exhaustion, and gratitude that you weren't alone.

30. AZZIE

I CAN'T BELIEVE HOW YOU LOOKED AT ME WHEN I TOLD YOU I'D killed a man before Dr. Phillips. Surprise, I expected that. Swept away by forlorn compassion? No.

Don't remember how long I've been in bed today. Only got up to type.

When I look up and go into my long dazes, different circles of color float above me.

And sometimes, I see Dr. Phillips' open, unseeing eyes.

Starting to care less if you catch the words I'm writing, if you judge me. Maybe, in the end, I want you to judge me, to offer me a mirror to myself. Selfish? Perhaps.

The guilt hurts too much, but it feels even more selfish to bring it up. In the end, you have a reason to hate me after what I did, after these unimaginable losses. Reasons.

You must grieve safety. Are we ever safe? The bed, where we scrubbed and scrubbed at the blood. As we wait to see if anyone suspects, if our lives are shattered. If I'm discovered and taken away to wherever the government disposes of Innsmouth folks.

I should be helping you more, but words are lost.

Though the dry air around me becomes less suitable for my condition, even as my skin peels and peels on the floor, I can't leave you. Perhaps it'd be kinder than you going to town and bringing back bags of salt.

Because of what I did to you, I need to stay. Let you have the satisfaction of caring for me, that routine. I'll molt to my wick if I need to.

You might grow to love the schedule, the sense of purpose, more than me.

Last time I was outside, it was mid-April, and spring was well underway as dogwoods released their clouds of white petals on the ground.

Yet it had started to snow. I reached my tongue out, and the coolness of the flakes was a brief respite. But not enough. You took my hand in yours, clasping it atop your knee.

Or daydream. We can build our castles in the air as Mina Murray and Lucy Westenra did in that gothic Victorian tale, whether we be soft or as salacious as a penny dreadful.

Except, when we become immortal, we'll never die.

I'll be immortal, and you...

If only I could be that for you. If only I was enough for you. For so long, you tentatively learned how to navigate your emotions and what you wanted. When to bow your head, when to hide. I imagine that was the key to your survival. You had to painstakingly anticipate what others wanted of you.

Meanwhile, though I did the same as a girl, I've tried to ignore my feelings. Acknowledging them and working through years of grief and damage would be too grueling.

You lost your mama, your virginity, your home, your son. How cruel would I need to be—me, this bulbous-eyed creature you've come to love —to abandon you after you've given me some semblance of life back?

Vin, I cannot leave you.

And if I don't go to the ocean soon, I will die. I feel it.

In the dead of night, last night, a grim acceptance washed over me. Never would I believe my death would hurt more than your son's, than all the other grief you must feel every day. Yet I can't make myself give you another person to mourn.

So, I'm at a loss.

Do you know me, have I let you? Is this person you know, this person who's betrayed you, me or a ghost I've offered? The bastard, walking around in me—this residue. Do I have any right to be me? My voice is me, and isn't. The woman in the mirror is me, she was at one point, but I haven't been her. Wasn't her for twelve years. Whenever she starts to look familiar, she grows unrecognizable.

Who's inside me? Sometimes I remember what he had me do. My stomach churns, and I think it might not be so bad to become a different species altogether, to swallow the salt and fade into the black. Or to travel to reaches he couldn't fathom.

I don't know how much longer I can last.

For you, I'll try.

31. VIN

No matter what I tried, your lips were chapped and bled easily; though I'd given you salted water, you threw up so much that you were dehydrated. I couldn't even get your appetite up for lobster; eventually, everything you ate, you couldn't keep down. I tried.

You tried, too. Oh, you tried, humiliated and fighting despondency.

You withered in front of me.

When it rained, if you had enough energy, sometimes you'd go and sit in it. I tried to tell you once that it might not be healthy, to spend so long outside, but you didn't budge. Your head hung, and I feared you would die right there. So, I went out and held your scaled, webbed hand.

You were dying.

May arrived, and rain relentlessly beat against the shutters. I sat on the hearth by the fire as you came into the room.

"Why are you really helping me?" you asked, at a distance.

It seemed like a ridiculous question. You needed me, so I was there. "Because I care."

Solemn, soft, you asked, "What about before, when this hell first started?"

"I'm repaying you," I said, continuing to stare into the flames. "Helping you after you helped me."

You released a sad sigh. "I understand, but you don't need to repay me. Ever."

"I can try," I said hoping that'd be the end of it.

Your voice was strained. "Is that it? Or is this work to distract you, like my job was for me?"

We both knew something: You stayed for me. In my selfish dependence on you for self-worth, I was letting you suffer; I let you languish and accept half-treatments to delay the inevitable.

In those books you had, what few novels had women who loved women, I saw their fates. Separation. Death. Suicide. Inevitable doom and tragedy.

And I had the horrible thought that you stayed because you thought that you must suffer, that this was some twisted repentance.

This would be different, I said. We live in a cosmos where alien beings take the faces and hands of men as disguises and give life to children and colors beyond human conception. Where immortality is more than a fantasy of medieval chemists. Endless possibilities. If our fathers could transform themselves with callous disregard, why couldn't we transcend ourselves with love?

And at times, you expressed a need for my comfort, so I thought our dependence must be mutual. I was able to excuse it.

Lumbering and hunched over, you joined me on the hearth. "I'm not judging you for it."

Irritation stirred in me. "Hm. It sounds like you are."

You inhaled, and your gills contracted. "I only want us to be honest with each other. And maybe, if I know how you feel, it makes this all easier."

I didn't look directly at your face. If I did, I feared I'd cry. "Makes what easier? Dealing with the pain or staying with me?"

A pause. "I don't know."

I rubbed my temple, not able to remember the last time I slept. "Can't argue right now." Of course, I was part of the tension. Searching for the right words, I said, "I don't know what I'd do without you, but..." You rubbed your throat and slid away, standing shakily. I thought you were leaving. "But if I'm only making your suffering worse by making you stay here, we should..."

My heart squeezed when, falling to your knees in front of me, you rested your head on my knee. Tentatively, I pressed my fingers to your scalp, the prickly skin growing slick. You liked that, when I rolled my thumb against your head, and I imagined that you never had the chance for that kind of affection at home. "It's not your fault this is happening."

Your laugh was more of a wet cough. "Sure. Guess that doesn't really matter, in the end."

Reluctantly, I left you there, went to the nightstand and pulled out the drawer, the pearl easing to greet me. As I returned, I took it out and rolled it between my fingers. I sat back down, and you again pressed your cheek into my knee, my gown hitched up.

"I do want to stay with you. I want to make everything up to you. I…" You trailed off, eyelids drooping.

My chest burned. "And I want what's best for you." Even if it killed me.

Dr. Phillips' death remained a pall over us, that reminder that you'd have to hide, have to disappear from the world in one way or another. This way was the most excruciating. You could afford to let your work go, maybe I could fill in. And I did, in the end.

It was me keeping you from healing and recovery.

And soon, small bouts of regretted irritation might become a simmering resentment. If it weren't for me, you could go. Like that Barrett Browning poem about grief. It wouldn't be the emotional overtures that killed us, but those long silences. Those pains we started to hide because they became numb. *Touch it; the marble eyelids are not wet: / If it could weep, it could arise and go.*

I thought you'd drifted off, but when I looked down, our eyes met.

I murmured, trying to keep my voice from trembling, "I think you should go into the sea to complete your transformation, and go and look for your mother."

Your voice was small. "What if Mother's dead?"

I pressed both my hands on your shoulders, keeping in mind not to do it too hard. "You won't know if you don't look."

You shut your eyes. "Maybe the possibility of her being alive is better than knowing for certain she's gone. And I'm grown, so I don't need to chase after her."

"Mothers matter, even after their children are older." I suck in a whistling breath through my nose. "Knowing Wilbur is dead is harder than not knowing, but that's not easy, either. If you imagine the best, you can imagine the worst, too." The bombs, the government "detainment facilities." I couldn't keep you from finding out. It'd be cruel. "And I suppose I know what I'm dealing with. Before, I couldn't face what happened with him because I didn't know."

"And you can face it now."

"Yes. I don't know how I feel." I rubbed an eye with my sleeve. "Numbness. Dunno. Guess it'll pass." At the time, I didn't know if things would get better or worse. In the short run, the numbness was better than despair, and my life did improve in aching steps. I'd be lying if I said grief was easy.

Against my skin, you said, so tired, "I don't want you to go through that alone, but I'm damned useless knowing how to talk about these things. You know that. And the last thing I want to do is make it worse."

"You aren't."

"I already did," you croaked.

I rubbed into the base of your skull. "And with me here, you'll get worse because you feel obligated to stay."

"It's not only an obligation, Vin."

"What could it be?" I asked.

Your eyes snapped up at me. "You don't know?"

A pause. "We've only known each other for six months."

"Epics have been made about less."

Swallowing, I shook my head. "I don't want my story to be an epic. After all that's happened, I want quiet and peace." Something I was told was impossible after what I'd been through. Unvirginal girls didn't have happy endings. The only good heroines are girls, such as Alice in the land of evil queens.

You curled your hands to your chest. "I only wanted to spend my life here, move on from the past."

Knowing you might leave, I thought I'd scream and shout. Something might break, like how you accidentally crushed that glass when I told you the full story about what Papa did.

But if you were to stay here, how many more of your teeth could I grind down? Until they were all dull, as your pain worsened. As you became a ghost for me.

Together, our bones were heavy. The fire warming my back, I lowered my lips, and before they pressed against your feverish, sweat-damp brow, I'd already made my decision.

I pulled away and met your eyes, a resignation leadening the air.

You'd made yours, too.

32. VIN

THE NIGHT CARRIED A CHILL, AND A LIGHT SNOW FELL. WE never shared a summer together, did we?

My driving was much slower than yours, but we met little traffic. You laid yourself in the back under one of your shawls, so no one would see you.

When we parked off the road, we hurried to the ocean, shadows under the glowering moon.

And a poem hung in my mind, like the hammock I curled into once the days grew warmer.

Frankly I wish I were dead. My throat grew taut. *When she left, she wept / a great deal; she said to me, "This parting must be / endured, Sappho. I go unwillingly."*

Your bottom lip trembled.

If you forget me, think of our gifts to Aphrodite / and all the loveliness that we shared / all the violet tiaras, braided rosebuds, / dill and crocus twined around your young neck / myrrh poured on your head / and on soft mats girls with / all that they most wished for beside them.

As we went down the incline, our feet touched the beach. We were completely alone, except for one another. As soon as we reached flatness, and my heart seized as I saw the water, you stopped. You wore trousers and an altered shirt that exposed your growing fin.

"Hold on." You crouched on the sand with a huff. "I need to rest."

I didn't know if you were stalling, but I wouldn't question you. I knelt with you. We didn't touch or say anything for several minutes. The wind was low and warm, but I didn't feel its comfort. Your breaths were labored, gurgling deep in your throat, but your expression was blank.

"I can't believe it's been six months," you murmured.

"It feels much longer," I said. Not long enough.

With a sharp movement of your head, you said, "I was going to say it feels too short. All my life has felt like it slips away too fast." With a deep breath, you looked up, the moonlight filling your green eyes. "I can try to bring you back things here, a quahog pearl as purple as lavender. Yes, I can bring you back a pearl, but not like that other one. A violet one, like your eyes."

Hollow and possessing no other words, I said, "I don't want gifts. I only want you."

Snapped out of your dream, you grimaced. "Please don't."

I shook my head. No reproach. Only fatigue. "Don't make it difficult?"

That time had long passed. I didn't want you to feel guilty, but I couldn't hide the heaviness behind my eyes. All pretensions had fallen away, even those I didn't know I had.

"I wish I could've been honest with you from the start. I, I wish..."

I touched your elbow. "After all you've done, it doesn't matter to me if you have some secrets. Everyone does. I want to ask if you've ever had something you want to tell me, but it's not something we can force."

I meant it. Had we time, I wanted to learn everything, but I respected the boundaries we had set either aloud or with a tacit contract.

You sharply inhaled. "I suppose this is it." Abruptly, you stood and strode toward the water. My world slowed to a crawl.

Too soon, you met the sea like an old lover.

This was it.

A lump formed in my throat as the full moon outlined you, and the water lapped at your trousers, up to your knees. I lurched up, fearing you'd disappear under the waves. That I'd call and call and call you, but you'd continue to descend and, like with your sickness, I could only watch.

Moving fast, I waded into the shallows, going to your side.

"You have to understand, I was scared," you said, continuing what we'd been talking about, as if we hadn't stopped. You fully faced me, and I was shocked that tears glistened on your cheeks.

"If I know anything, it's fear." Even after all these years, I haven't forgotten what it means to be afraid; but I also haven't forgotten how to be brave.

"My father was this man who had the walk of a wolf, and he had this beard the color of iron. I look a lot like him, except for the eyes. And of course, the scales. And the gills."

"Oh. He didn't have gills?"

We shared a meager laugh.

"Those are all Mother."

You scratched at your arm, but since we got into the water, more color flooded your cheeks and the scaly hollow of your throat. "Every day, he locked himself in his study. Once he started, sometimes he'd go past dinner, and I learned to eat alone. He endlessly read books about the occult and esoteric things I didn't understand."

My mouth grew dry. "Like my papa."

Your eyes darkened, and so did the lines around them. "Yes, and he always had men over, men who I believe were part of some strange cult he had. He even gave himself a special name: Kamog. I was meant to be kept away. But when I would spy on them, they all spoke to one another in what I thought were nonsense languages because they made these sounds that I'd never heard before."

You paused, then continued:

"My father was inside my body for twelve years, since I was thirteen. Do you know what I mean? He killed himself and put his soul in my body, and then shoved my soul out."

That knocked the breath from my lungs. "He, he what?"

"I suppose I've thought about it so much, I don't think about how it sounds. He found a way to put his soul into my body, but to do that, he needed a vessel to swap mine into. So, he drove one of his own antique swords through his body, and he left me inside his corpse."

I didn't know what to say, but I supposed nothing was an answer, an answer that I was going to let you speak.

"After I got my body back...I was absent from it all those years. I wish I could explain what it's like to have all those years and years of my life I only remember through him, like watching my body act on a cinema screen. These memories aren't mine, but I remember doing them. Or having them done to me."

"Your soul was in his body for that long? Where..."

"Yes. In his corpse. First, rotting in an attic. Then under the ground in his pine coffin."

My throat closed up in shock. All that time rotting underground in the pitch blackness. In your dead father's body because of his evil magic. I wanted to ask why, but I held back. Maybe because, in the end, whether it was perversion or your father's desperate need for recognition or his scientific hunger or, most likely, a nauseous mix of all three, it didn't matter.

The results were the same. Your stories, your motivations. Those matter. All that's left of him is what he gave you. What he left you to cope with in his scientific greed and heartlessness.

Instead, I said nothing, so you could tell me everything without interruption.

"He superimposed his soul into my body, so he could use it as he wished. And he left me to suffer in the utter horror of complete darkness, left me to the stench of earth and his own mouldering body." Your lips thinned, your eyes dark and furious. "That was all I was good for, a burning conflagration of meat and chine bone he could navigate as long as it suited him. Until he could find another 'superior' male body that suited him better. For that, he needed to find a man to seduce as him, as me. And I escaped. My soul did. His own body crumbled to dust, bones drifted away from the joints. Old and decayed and loosened by worms. And I was free. Found myself in the air. Floating in a haze outside of everything. A bouquet of yellow flowers on a nearby tombstone, a sobbing man I didn't recognize several graves away. All this blue underworld."

Strange to think that was something you, always grounded and pragmatic, had endured. I imagine it's what the Yith feel, those creatures from beyond that need a host to live ever since a horrific tragedy displaced them. For you, always grounded, it must've been a nightmare. No ground firm under your feet. The air, the water, we must always adjust to the harsh world.

Your voice became hoarse, a croak in the crooning ocean. "I found him. No, I found her, this." Your webbed hands glided in front of your body. Over your heart. "The puppet he used. Me, a woman attending university. A wedding ring on one finger, my throat just newly strangled, and soulless. Left to mold in a cellar. A ghostly pallor, some rigor mortis in the muscles, but not yet decomposed."

A long stretch of silence as your gums and throat revolted against you, your hand pressed to your mouth as bloody saliva dripped down. I waited, eyes pricked with tears. This poor woman.

If I sobbed right there, it wouldn't only be grief; it'd be righteous fury. I better understood your wrath when Dr. Phillips turned the gun on me. Or your promises that Papa would never hurt me again.

You continued, "Apparently, from what I gained from notes around that estate, despite being a conveniently nearby vessel for his ritual, I wasn't a good enough body for him. Too weak. Small. Female. So, he married a man in the hopes of using him as a host instead. But Edward found out. He killed that Asenath, my father, my body, and tossed the body away. Me." Your voice cracked, wet, and you swallowed. "But you see, that was perfect for Father. That was his plan, for my body to die. He now had a freshly inert vessel to store Edward's soul in as he took over his body." You darkly smirked. "But before he could complete his plan, I entered my own body again."

I was afraid to ask more, but this would be the only chance I could. "What happened to Edward?"

Your expression fell. "I don't know. I regret it, to think his soul was a casualty in a fight he couldn't help. That he's lingering in the cosmos somewhere. He murdered his own wife, inflicted wounds on my body that I dealt with weeks after. But my father hunted him. It wasn't right, that in killing one man, the one I meant to gladly murder, I killed two."

When you paused, I realized that you waited for a reaction. But my reaction was stunned silence. And then, a soft question. "How did you do it?"

When you told me, your expression was flat at first. "It's like I said in the woods. I shot him six times." You scoffed. "You should've seen the look on his face." Solemnly, you corrected yourself, "'Edward's' face when he saw me back in my own body. I wonder how I must've looked to him. I think I must've been enraged. And he was so desperate for a 'real' body, a man's body, that he never expected me to leave his snare."

I asked, "You killed him. Shot him. But what stopped him from taking over another body, switching to someone else while he was in the corpse?"

"There's one weakness to the process: cremation. A gunshot, a knife— the soul can survive those, but if a body burns and is completely destroyed, the soul dies with it. Father was quick, but not quick enough. I sneaked into the crematorium with his body in the trunk of Edward's auto. And I watched the body he stole crumble to ash. A howl, his scream, his soul disintegrating. If there is something like the hells in certain mythologies, I'd like to think that was the sound of him being sucked into one of them."

"I'm glad he's dead. That you were able to get back what he took." That he won't torment you in person when the mental anguish, his legacy, is enough of a haunt.

Your lips shook. "But have I, have I truly?"

"Yes," I insisted firmly. "Absolutely. Thinking otherwise will drive you mad."

Your voice shook and shook. "This body. It, it, I was his for so long, and once I almost grew used to it, might've come to, to, to accept it, it changed. This isn't the body he took."

My reply was fierce. "No, it's yours." And had we an eternity, perhaps you would say, in some small way your body's gifts were mine, happily shared. Since we had no time, I needed to get my words across. "Your old body, how you were before, how you are now, this is all you. Azzie. My pearl."

Desperation crept into your tone. "And what about my smoking cigars or how I dress. All the ways I'm different? All my masculine proclivities?"

"He has no claim over those. You liked many of those things when you were a child. Those are you, still. Not him."

"Yes, but it all becomes so fuzzy. What is me, and what is this—this residue."

I said with urgency, rage, love, "I don't see a trace of him in you." People make themselves ghosts to us. I saw your father as that. A ghost of yours. Not you. You weren't what he did to you.

A tear ran silver down your cheek. "I want you to know I never meant to treat your sons like they weren't a part of you. I only didn't understand. I thought if we burned the past, it meant it couldn't haunt us. I wanted you to thrive, Vin. Not mourn all your life. I was ignorant."

I couldn't blame you, and I don't. "We've both been learning this whole time." I leaned and kissed the corner of your mouth, closed my eyes, took a deep breath, and inhaled the salt of you. With a sudden intake of breath, you pulled me into a hug, head against my shoulder.

How miraculous to live, to live after horror and think, oh, what a strange, wide, but beautiful cosmos we live in. And how strange to live in a cosmos of uncaring gods' machinations, and yet I found compassion and hope in East Providence.

That somehow made our bond rare, more precious than if there were loving gods. Some conspired to drive mortals mad for the fun of it like wily Nyarlathotep, and others, like my so-called husband, the gate-and-key, had no rhyme or reason to his actions.

Even in the horror and chaos, we aren't devoid of love. The gods might be, but we aren't. And in a way, that's a power they cannot grasp.

In the water, though, I didn't think of miracles. The sea, the sand, the world, they all were barren of them. Rather than a universe of endless wonders and secrets, we faced a linear path, like the girl in the red hood with her paths of pins and needles, but there was only one, and it was going down.

I clung to you, your head on my collarbone. You lost composure, sobbing openly, making warbling, wet sounds against my black dress. Against my chest, your pulse beat rapidly in your neck. My hands molded to your shoulder, those bumpy but smooth scales, and above your hip. I pulled you closer, and my eyes stung and overflowed.

No matter how cold the water was, I didn't feel the chill. We were crystallized in the moment foolishly thinking it could last. And for a long time, too brief, we didn't part.

33. VIN

I watched you leave, after, the last of your head submerged in the water. My fingers ached as they remembered the last time they stroked your scalp.

Fifteen years.

Fifteen years of quiet here. Not in the world, but here in this little cottage I come to after sorting files and perhaps going to the bookstore or Lourenço's with my handful of friends. It feels like cheating, sometimes. I once weighed my life with how much pain and conflict I endured.

The first night I was alone in the cottage, I fell asleep with my cheek against the window and dreamed of an alien shore with blue, phosphorescent mushrooms that dappled the silver-leaved trees.

The cats played, the wind rustled the grass, and there was peace. I have my books and my friends, and I feel full enough. A hurricane ruined the oyster population of the Gansett. Lourenço's began serving wine with its cuisines after the repeal of the prohibition of alcohol. The second world war ended, with the Paris Peace Treaties signed last year.

This is where the story should stop. The bittersweet end to a relationship between two women, like in the novels. The kinds that are converted into cinema. One woman dies poetically by walking into the ocean, and another gets married to a man and has his children.

Or stays alone. Or kills herself, too. I've had time to think about these things.

Crying against her mama's freckled shoulder, Persephone says goodbye to the sunflowers and mosquitoes of summer, and Eurydice droops by the Styx and counts ghost teeth in the loam. Those who suffer are destined to go mad, the myths say. Poseidon rapes Medusa; she becomes a monster; and she must be slain while pregnant and alone in her cave of pearls and statues.

If I were a princess in a poem, if I was allowed to be anything but a villain, I might die in a boat or throw myself off a seacliff. How poetic to die in your domain. A comfortable ending, the most final kind for pariahs.

This is how things should be. Your need for distance stood opposite of my need for closeness, and yet—

I stand by the ocean often. Sometimes, for hours.

I've worked to distance myself from someone who makes me happy, as if you're incompatible with the rest of what I love. As if love is singular. As if our world is one of stark blacks and whites, this one where gods roam and people swap their souls and women can live in the sea.

You learned it isn't weak to need help, and I learned how to fend for myself. Ah. But the thing is, I'd already done that. I only refused to see that in myself, hated myself for being alive and leaving what I thought was my purpose. I was wrong to think being a daughter, godswife, and mother were all I was good for. My old life hurt me, and yet it was all I knew.

But that doesn't mean I don't want love. A family, whatever that looks like, even if it's friends and a partner. Wrong as I was to think those roles were all that would make me worth something, that I needed to cling to what I could get, that doesn't mean I can't have love.

To be strong, to survive, I must be alone. Whole and alone. A noble martyr to live a life not too controversial or fulfilling. Or entwined with someone and dependent. With someone or whole on my own.

A lie.

A lie since I came home with your clothes in the passenger's seat. And I lifted it up to inhale the smell, that remaining part of you, and I realized this fear in me that your presence would fade from your clothes, your furniture, and your sheets.

I told myself I left your clothes alone because I was moving on, and touching them would only tempt me to linger in memories, languish like I was used to doing. When memories are all I've had, they were dangerous and volatile. So I believed.

If I tried too hard to find that unique pair of woodsmoke and cinnamon I smelled when I first woke up here, I'd lose myself, that elusive me I was building and rebuilding over and over. I'd grieve, as if grief must be shunned.

Our Only Autumn Together, I wrote atop the beginning of your words before banishing them from sight, so I could avoid them.

No. *Our First Autumn Together.*

I'm not afraid to read your words anymore, so I have. Right down to the last.

Again.

Yours.

Azzie, I do want to see you again.

We will see each other again. When we do, we'll know each other more than ever before.

I've grieved so much, and I'm damned tired of it. We don't need to have our idyllic walks in East Providence. I can walk with you by the cove at night. You can come to the cottage, and I'll kiss your scales as the radio murmurs to us by the heart, as fireflies burst coronas in the dark with their love-waltzes.

Years ago, during the war, I read in the papers the sad fate of a woman, a writer named Virginia Woolf, who filled her overcoat with stones and drowned. After hearing of her passing, I read a story she wrote for a female lover, *Orlando*. Where she wrote in melancholy, *I'm sick to death of this particular self. I want another.* It reminded me of myself.

It reminded me of you. And endings.

Together, we'll rewrite every tragedy. After all, in this cosmos full of gods and immortals, someone like Orlando could exist.

How odd to think what it'll be like. I've lived over half a century already, and Deep Ones can live forever, can't they? I imagine you taking care of me when I'm ninety years old, roving the brush through my hair, your webbed hand gently holding mine, minding the high knobby rivers protruding on top of them.

The things I could tell you about. How I walk the streets often in the evening. John the barber. Sergio at Lourenço's. Rebecca at City Hall, who I kissed twice.

Everyone recognizes me. How, on a whim, I took money I saved up and booked a train to Atlanta, a place with its own ghosts, watching the hills and trees and water pass me by. North Carolina, Tennessee, Georgia. New lands I thought I'd be dead before I could even consider seeing them.

And the things you could tell me about. What the cities at the bottom of the sea are like, who lives there, how your mother is doing.

I remember a poem in one of your collections, the one with the metaphysical verses. About two lovers apart, comparing them to a drawing compass:

> If they be two, they are two so
> As stiff twin compasses are two;
> Thy soul, the fixed foot, makes no show
> To move, but doth, if the other do.
> And though it in the center sit,
> Yet when the other far doth roam,
> It leans and hearkens after it,
> And grows erect, as that comes home.
> Such wilt thou be to me, who must,
> Like th' other foot, obliquely run;
> Thy firmness makes my circle just,
> And makes me end where I begun.

Except, we won't end in the beginnings of us, the ones written for us; we'll begin anew, on that day you saved me from drowning and, soaking wet, we laughed on the sand.

I'm ready to go out to the auto and drive to the beach. You'd be impressed with how my driving has improved.

This is how we meet again.

Rather than ending on our parting, we will join again in that very water. On that cool sand, I'll listen for your footsteps with the crisp wind in my hair. Alone, I'll imagine our last kiss. Our slow, long nights with our legs threaded together.

Again, I'll re-teach myself the language of us, dreaming of the syllables of your fins under my thumb, as I trace each dip.

Amid the taste and scent of the sea, I'll dance to the cadence of your green eyes softly lingering on me. I'll pine after it and, before doubt seeps in, smell your salt and tobacco. I'll wade into the water, pockets absent of stones.

I'll turn around. Yes. I'll turn around. See you in all your splendor. Smile, weep tears of joy, and think:

There you are.

I am home.

Love,
    Vin

34. Azzie

I cannot wait to meet and know you again.

Yours,
    Azzie

35. Letter from Robert L. Phelps to His Friend, Howard West, 1958

Dear Howard,

Thank you for writing. I am happy to hear that Constance is recovering well from her mastectomy. I wish I could tell you more about myself. Times have been hard. Day after day at the cannery. With any luck, the recession will cease soon. I'm hoping the writing has gone well. How are the magazine sales?

Anyhow, you'll never believe the happenings here in East Providence. Have you read the paper? I'm unsure if news will travel far and not simply be dismissed as local folklore or a madman's ramblings.

It's well known that throughout the more remote areas of Rhode Island and Massachusetts, there are a great deal of legends. Most are old and only truly believed by the crazed inbred trash in the hills. However, ever since I heard on the radio about that creature that attempted to steal a book from Miskatonic, and all the past silence around Innsmouth, I've realized that the malaise I've been feeling might not be remnants from the war, and what was left of the Spanish and Russian commies at Mauthausen, but dark portents I can't name.

Though East Providence is very modern, there are plenty of people who live on the outskirts and along the stretch of beach. Since the 1500s, there have been reports about creatures being seen on the shores. I always thought they were remnants of those ghost tales about ships lost at sea.

But in the last few months, I've noticed people lingering on the edges of town, always wearing black. I suspected they were federal agents, but why? Could it be connected to the continued tabloid stories about camps for people who might've been in Innsmouth during the prohibition raid.

Yeah, those folks were always strange and ugly as sin, and they smelled awful, at least according to my cousin who had the unfortunate task of doing census reports there, but I can't imagine what could've been so terrible that their home was wiped off the map. I don't think that the government would kill a town for its smell, even if it might've done us all a favor.

It's all odd to me, all that bombing and hush-hush over a rum operation. And attacking the reef outside the town? Eisenhower might do better to direct all his efforts toward reducing costs.

You will likely mock me for what I tell you, but believe me when I say with utmost seriousness: The rumors from those blasted rags are true. I don't know if they are keeping the Innsmouth people in camps, though it's certainly not a new government practice, but those stories about fish-people—the "Deep Ones" according to the few documents from Innsmouth's ruins that were found by some intrepid reporter—are real.

I saw one myself.

First came the whispers about a fish-creature stalking the shores, but only at night. What was strangest wasn't that. Again, these legends float about, even if only the insane, I thought, believed in them. To think I might be going mad with what I've heard. My eyes have never lied, however.

The woman I'll mention, her name was Lavinia, and apparently she was well-liked but reclusive. She had starkly white hair and purple eyes that were pink in direct sunlight. She often wore bright colors, but always the cool sorts. Purple, blue, green. She took a liking to green. As of late, one could see her sauntering down Agnes Street with a cane. I've heard she spoke right, she was no halfwit, but had a bumpkin kind of an accent.

She apparently spent much time near the ocean. No surprise. I find only the very young or very old care much about the ocean and believe in the mysticism surrounding it. My friend, I'm starting to think they had the whole of it.

A buddy of mine caught wind of a raid on the cottage where the old bird lived. Now, why on earth would you need to break down the door of a lonesome senior's house? What could she have done, cracked some fool's head open with her stick? It was a huge bluster, and despite whatever Mr. J. Edgar Hoover had planned, almost everyone within a couple of miles flocked to the bust and saw something they weren't supposed to. Naturally, we took a ride to that little cottage with our guns.

When the men in black suits burst into the cottage, apparently no one had the best view, especially not myself. All they saw was one of the agents pause before something massive burst out. It was some hideous fish-frog creature with bulbous green eyes and a woman in its arms. Lavinia. You might imagine that we had our sights on that thing, but we didn't want to shoot an old woman. In retrospect, maybe death would've been a mercy. And yet, the old bat didn't act like she was in danger.

Did you ever see that 1954 picture about that repulsive creature who lusts after a woman in a lagoon? That's what I had in my head, but the thing wasn't so massive, and its form was bent. Its unspeakable eyes took up most of its head, and its teeth were long inside its large, ghastly mouth. It looked more like a toad in some parts than a fish-man. Instead of hulking around, it held an unnatural grace as it raced through the woods. Meanwhile, instead of screaming for help, the old woman clung to the monster for dear life. One would think you would try to flee, twist around like a worm. Scream. But then again, Providence girls are known for being rather queer.

Before you ask, yes, those who saw her most clearly said the woman was alive and that she acted almost exasperated at the attempts to pacify the creature while saving the woman.

The agents, about six of them, pursued, while others drove to the Crook Point Bascule Bridge, where the thing apparently took Lavinia and dove into the Seekonk, which leads into the Providence and, eventually, Gansett Bay.

They searched and searched the water for a drowned woman, but Lavinia's body was never found. Some say as they saw a flash of green hit the water, they went blind with a flash of white light, but not at once. The sky above, which was dark with approaching storm clouds, suddenly became lighter and lighter, until a dazzling light exploded into life for only a second.

I'm not sure what I believe, but I think those two are still out there. Apparently, long ago, there was another woman with Lavinia at the cottage who acted very secretively, and there were rumors that both ladies might be part of the Old Free-Will Church, those crazies in the hills and stony churches who talk about outer gods or something I might've thought was nonsense before.

However, the other woman went missing a long time ago, like others since before even the Great War, like that doctor. I wonder if Old Lady Lavinia had been sacrificing them to the monster or whatever heathen gods she worships, like those yokels who say they worship a modern avatar of Cybele.

Allegedly, Old Lady Lavinia had been living with the monster, the Deep One, for a while, doing whatever unholy deeds that hillbilly cultists do with monsters of the depths. You know, at Innsmouth, it's rumored the men were forced to wed sea-beasts who'd beget their disgusting progeny.

The people spin stories now. About how the old woman would take plates of lobster and place them in the sand. And one time, when fog obscured most of the shore, the monster came, and the old woman shook with fear and wept, but confusingly, she set her forehead to its scaly one. Before, I thought those stories were to scare children away from the ocean, but now, I'm only shocked it took so long to try to apprehend them.

Whatever they were, I suppose they'll haunt the ocean together. Sure as hell I won't be swimming in it soon.

Take care, and send Constance my love.

Kind regards,
Rob

. . .

P.S. Of course, I'm sure I don't need to tell you, but don't tell a soul, not even Constance. I heard the people at the scene who got caught up by the feds got a good deal of hush money under threat of a nightly visit where, after, their family might never be able to find them again.

And if Old Lady Lavinia is indeed a witch, who knows what curses she and her sea monster might weave upon us.

ABOUT THE AUTHOR

Morgan is a horror, fantasy, and romance author. They have a soft spot for all things dark and gothic, especially vampires and an array of castle-dwelling monsters. They've also never written an angel that they didn't want to make at least little weird-looking. Their other recent works are *A Flame in the Night* and *Witch Soul*. More about their work can be found at morgandante.com.

Made in United States
Troutdale, OR
06/22/2024

20742195R00120